ME TOO, MY FRIEND

By:
Anabel LeFrancois

Bookman Publishing & Marketing
Martinsville, Indiana
www.Bookmanmarketing.com

© Copyright 2003, Anabel LeFrancois

All Rights Reserved.
No part of this book may be
reproduced, stored in a retrieval system, or transmitted by any
means, electronic, mechanical, photocopying, recording,
or otherwise, without written permission from the author.

ISBN: 1-932301-63-1

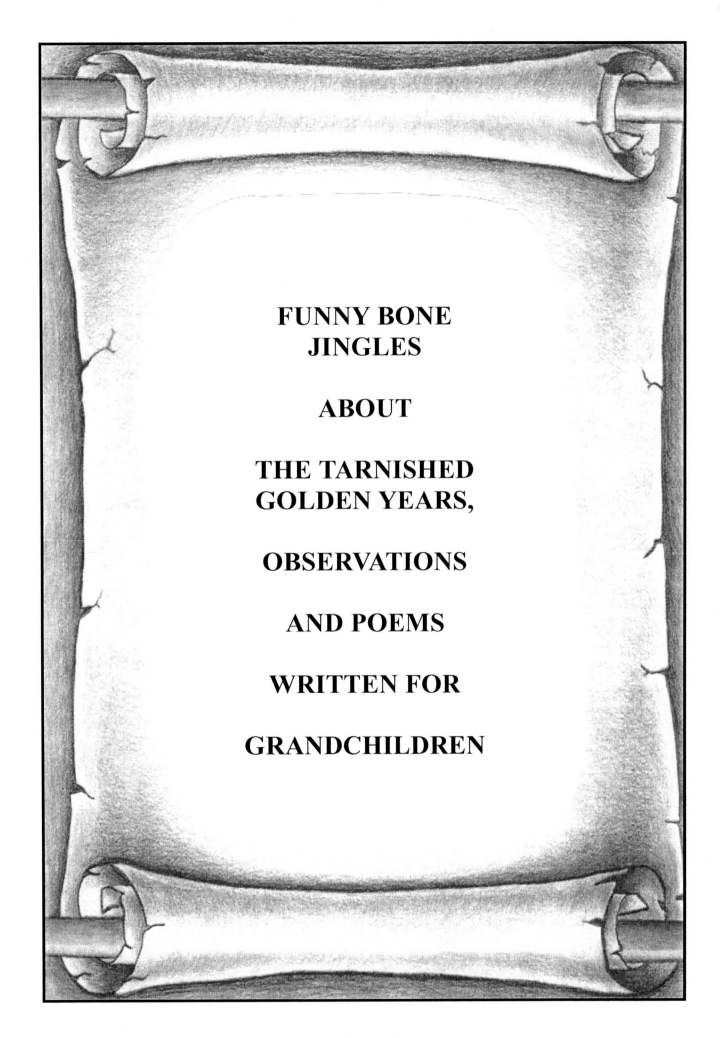

FUNNY BONE JINGLES

ABOUT

THE TARNISHED GOLDEN YEARS,

OBSERVATIONS

AND POEMS

WRITTEN FOR

GRANDCHILDREN

ME TOO, MY FRIEND

the poet turns
his pulsing soul
quite inside out,
he shows the whole;

and souls that are inhibited
identify with parts of it.

Those thoughts
that can't get to the lips
are shared within
sweet comradeship

and minds can blend,
Me too, my friend

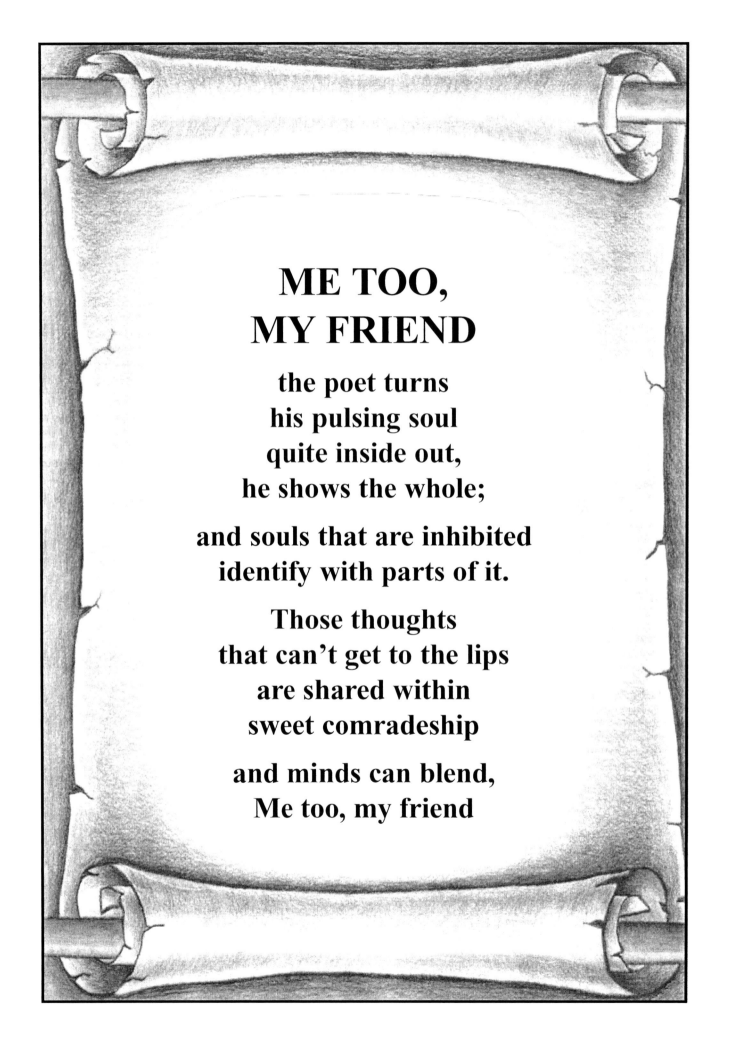

DEDICATED
TO
EVERYONE
WITH
LOVE
MY FAMILY
MY FRIENDS
MY PEERS

BY ANABEL

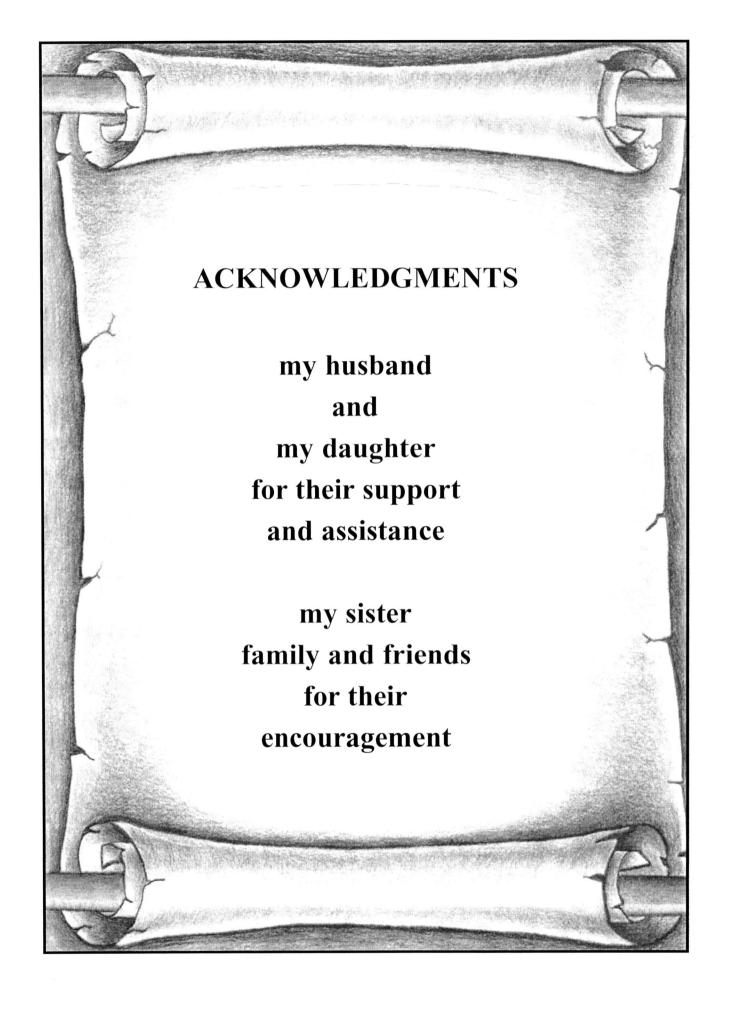

ACKNOWLEDGMENTS

my husband
and
my daughter
for their support
and assistance

my sister
family and friends
for their
encouragement

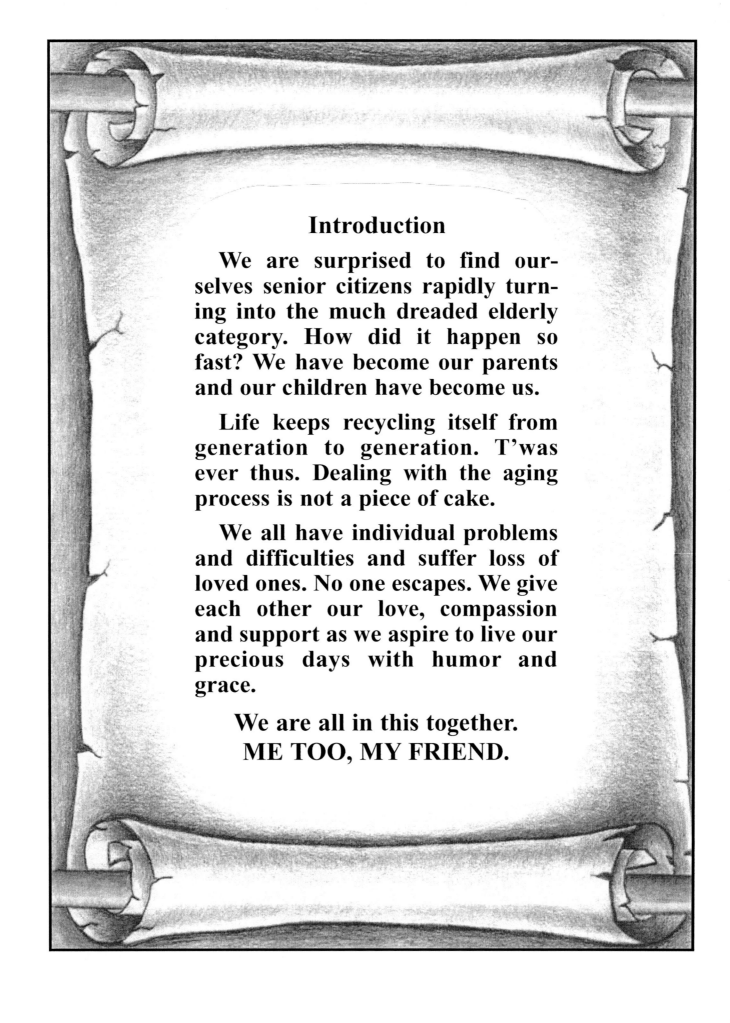

Introduction

We are surprised to find ourselves senior citizens rapidly turning into the much dreaded elderly category. How did it happen so fast? We have become our parents and our children have become us.

Life keeps recycling itself from generation to generation. T'was ever thus. Dealing with the aging process is not a piece of cake.

We all have individual problems and difficulties and suffer loss of loved ones. No one escapes. We give each other our love, compassion and support as we aspire to live our precious days with humor and grace.

We are all in this together.
ME TOO, MY FRIEND.

ME TOO, MY FRIEND

Anabel LeFrancois

AND THAT'S THE WAY IT IS . . .

I'm now an old lady,
my mirror tells the truth
all those birthday candles
have burned out my youth.

Should I write
my memoirs reviewing my past?
Pandora lids opened
would leave you aghast.
My life's been adventurous,
not boring or stale
but lack inclination
to write in detail.
Endeavors I tackled
were varied and wide,
ever chinning myself,
things had to be tried.

The things that were gutsy
I cherish the most.
When fate cruelly pushed me
from pillar to post
invented solutions
with moxie and pluck
then prayed my agenda
would not run amuck.
Ideas kept spawning,
some good and some bad,
just talk to my family
I almost drove mad.

Me Too, My Friend

I live with a passion,
with faith and with hope,
the world is my oyster,
it's foolish to mope.
I feel quite triumphant,
a phoenix am I
a lot more I'm planning to do
'fore I die.
The art of survival's
the name of the game.
It's alright to call me
a "spunky old dame."

Anabel LeFrancois

A BOOK IS BORN

The sculptor and his chisel
free statues trapped in stone.
I get these inspirations
demanding to be known,

so deep in the subconscious
a squirmy, tangled mess,
defy articulation,
a challenge, I confess.

So many ways of saying
ideas in my head,
perhaps I should be doing
something else instead.

Quite often I am stricken
with thoughts I can't resist.
I force them into jingles
that have a comic twist.

The task was really daunting
but after friendly taunting
my book is now completed.
I hope you'll want to read it.

Me Too, My Friend

BE GOOD TO YOURSELF

If my thoughts are intermingled
with some rhythm, wit and jingled
maybe spirits can be lightened
and a dreary day be brightened.

If you're really contemplating
that you could keep heaven waiting
doctors say that belly laughter
might postpone the feared hereafter.

When it comes to medication
humor has no limitation.
Fight the gloom and melancholy
treat yourself to fun and folly.

Do the things you relish doing.
Happiness deserves pursuing.

Anabel LeFrancois

LIVING THROUGH
A MAGNIFYING GLASS

I won't tell you how many glasses
of various strengths I own in the
performance of various duties.

I won't tell you how many magnifying
glasses are strategically placed
throughout the house.

I don't want to know how much time
is spent cleaning these things and
how much time is lost looking for
them. It takes tremendous focusing and
concentration since I am in perpetual
motion doing all the things I've always
done except drive a car.

Through a magnifying glass I learned the
computer and through a magnifying glass
I wrote and put this book together.
I am grateful for visual aids.
Like the pokey turtle I reach the finish
line. How much time it took matters not.

Me Too, My Friend

THE BEGINNER'S LAMENT

A little man lives in the right hand corner of my computer and he is too visible too much of the time. His elevator eyebrows are highly agitated, his eyeballs bulge and I get the feeling that he is scolding me with intuIts and a few swear words thrown in. He thinks I am making atrocious clicking decisions and I am responsible for his "hissy-fit." I call him Rasputin because he is always disputing my decisions. He's very vindictive. He agitates the printer to go on strike. He flashes instructions to do this and that and pretty soon the computer is frozen. I unfreeze it but then I get into a bewildering maze of instructions and I go to bed thinking I've broken it but hopeful that it will debug itself by morning. Rasputin thinks he's a trouble shooter but he's really a trouble maker because when he's not around everything's o.k. My daughter says she could banish him permanently but in spite of it all I like the human touch and "talking back" is good therapy. I calculate that with this prolific "state of the art" setup I'll be taking lessons the rest of my life. O.K. by me. I finally discovered that the computer, fast as it is, can only do one thing at a time so I am smarter than the computer because I can: pat my head and rub my stomach simultaneously.

Anabel LeFrancois

THE MANY FACES OF PATIENCE

PATIENCE is...
Silence
biting it's tongue.
Quiet endurance
tolerating distress.
Restraint finding serenity.
Calm Meditation
abandoning criticism.
Wisdom
resisting folly.
PATIENCE
is temper wearing an ice pack.
PATIENCE with one's self
is the hardest to come by.
PATIENCE had better make up
a good payroll.

I have deep admiration
for friends and acquaintances
who go through their
days, weeks, months and years
with humor and grace,
smiling through a veil
of nagging arthritic
aches and pains.

It takes an indomitable spirit
to keep pushing the limits
and not cave in to a
lethargic life style.

Me Too, My Friend

S-T-R-E-T-C-H

Now go to the cat
he knows where it's at.
He's undoubtedly smart
for he's mastered the art
of the leisurely s-t-r-e-t-c-h.
In your memory etch
the way he lays long
pulsating his song
that seems to beseech
a lengthier reach
to a body s-t-r-u-n-g out.
Here's what it's about....
coaxing muscles to yawn
by relaxing our brawn
proves slow motion is "real"
and gives time to "feel"
to taste the full measure
of this simple pleasure.

There's a lot more to say
but it's wrong to delay,
go straight to the cat,
he knows where its at
and you let him teach
the leisurely "reach"
till the skill becomes etched
and you're luxuriously s-t-r-e-t-c-h-e-d.

Anabel LeFrancois

CHEER UP,
THINGS COULD BE WORSE

No matter how the myth is garnished
those golden years are quickly tarnished.

That wrecking ball of nature's vengeance
soon strikes us all, robs independence.

Our body parts are prone to plague us,
the list of ailments is outrageous.

There's one good thought I must insert
be glad that wrinkles do not hurt.

A VERY DEEP THOUGHT

If the optimist gets the donut
and the pessimist gets the hole
the optimist gets heart attacks
and the pessimist low cholesterol.

THANKSGIVING

Each day is a new package
to be opened . . .
Twenty four hours
a separate piece of life
each different . . .
boxed up in a new day
laid end to end in groups of seven
to give us a full week
and then times four
plus two or three
to make a month
and all of this times twelve
to make a year.
Why isn't every day like Christmas?

Anabel LeFrancois

SLEEP

Low tide yawns
stroking echoes
banishing
meandering thoughts
to oblivion.

Sleep
insulating feelings,
releasing them
to roam and romp
their dreamland
freely.

Sleep
ushering drowsiness
interlude of caress
nestled in velvet
submission.

Sleep
edging into me
petitioning
faith glimmers
for tomorrow.

Me Too, My Friend

AWAKING

Awaking is stimuli needling
the subconscious
trespassing the domain of sleep
frisking dreams
nudging drowsiness
into consciousness.

Awaking should be
a pleasant coaxing
that takes it's time
to feel the new day's mood
and contemplate it's offerings.

Awaking in retirement
without the jolting shrillness
of the alarm clock
is a luxury indeed.
To be at liberty
to retreat under the covers
is a choice divine
and a dream come true.

Anabel LeFrancois

CONSIDERING

When I consider that my heart
without an interruption beat
since 1915 without fail
it's really an amazing feat

But when I lounge in quiet rest
I sometimes hear it's rhythmic pump
and have some apprehensive thoughts.
Is that an aggravated thump?

Could arteries be clogged and weak
my heart be working much too hard?
If I think about my age
reliance on my heart is jarred.

The medics say my heart's o.k.
should thank the Lord that I can hear.
The question lingers just how long
the pump is meant to persevere.

When I consider time that's left
for goals I've wanted to pursue
each morn I formulate my plans
then pray my body follows through.

Me Too, My Friend

DEALING WITH MY MORTALITY

When I have drawn my final breath
asleep in painless, peaceful death
I hope I leave things none the worse
for having trod this universe.

It's scary and I think I should
invent more ways of doing good
and pray the Lord my soul to take
or dying is a big mistake.

MORNING PRAYER

Last night I laid me down to sleep
I prayed the Lord my soul to keep.
This morning I got out of bed
relieved to know I am not dead.

Dear God please help me to get through
the day without a big snafu,
a fall, a heart attack, a stroke
or I'll be sorry I awoke.

Anabel LeFrancois

SPRING

Today I took a walk and saw a sight
that overwhelmed the soul of me.
I felt a tingling thrill
for over the fresh green floor
of a fenced in meadow
spring laid a thick shag rug
of flowering mustard
that looks to the sky and sun.
It stretches
from fence post to fence post
in quiet contentment
with the purpose of it's being;
which is to be
pregnant with the seed of life,
exquisitely beautiful to the eye
and cheerfully yellow.

I came home with fresh air thoughts,
happy that
Spring laid a thick shag rug
of flowering mustard
that looks to the sky and sun
so cheerfully yellow.

Me Too, My Friend

DENIAL

Mirror, Mirror on the wall
what a mystery you are
something weird is going on
that's confusing and bizarre.

I've concluded it is haunted
by another lady's face,
when I try to use my mirror
she invades my mirrored space.

I try hard to beat her to it
but she always gets there first.
Never get a glance of me,
could it be the mirror is cursed?

Mirror, Mirror on the wall
make your magic work for me,
please erase that other face
give me MY identity.

Anabel LeFrancois

THE DENTIST

Too often it's been happening
I'm sitting in the dentist chair.
Grim verdicts he's been rendering...
another tooth's beyond repair.

I've had my share of root canals
crowns, caps and partials followed next.
The years demand survival fees
and I keep writing bigger checks.

I wring my hands in deep despair
I fear I've no more teeth to spare.

A NO WIN

Some Days
you're the bug on the windshield
and
some days
you're the windshield.

-Unknown

Me Too, My Friend

ON MOWING THE LAWN

Grass
in suburbia
blading altitude,
cliquey in clumps,
crouching corners,
straddling borders
and boundaries,
spilling over,
resting growth
on forbidden territory.

Grass
promiscuous with foxtail,
dandelion
and assorted weeds
stealing nutrients
and chlorophyll
helter-skeltering
undisciplined.
I'm sorry
you cannot be a meadow.

Anabel LeFrancois

MY LUCKY HERITAGE

I had a mother
who sang off-key
cheerfully.

Everything she did
said "Life is what you make it."

She knew she sang off key
but she loved to sing
so she sang anyway.

She sparkled my days
with her jaunty off-keyness.

Mother's Penmanship Class 12-14-1906

Me Too, My Friend

**Mother's Penmanship Class
December 1906**

Anabel LeFrancois

LOSS

Give me a gypsy violin
playing a plaintive melody
in the background for this sad tale.

It was on my birthday in 1996
when I voluntarily surrendered
my drivers license.

The good news - One stress in my life has been eliminated
The bad news -   I am stranded in the country
The good news - I have more time to write
The bad news -   I lost my independence.

PARABLE OF COURAGE

Baby fistfuls
of bright green ribbon
have punctured thick asphalt
along the sides of the road.
SAD
Little thought is given to
these brave crabgrass resurrections.

Me Too, My Friend

FOR MACULAR DEGENERATES LIKE ME

We're the Merry Macs, we fight the fight
a-doing our thing with diminished sight. Dysfunctional read-
ers is what we've become magnifying glasses we hold till
we're numb.

We're the Merry Macs, Hurrah for us!
We put on a smile as we ride the bus.
To the brightness of sunlight our eyes don't adjust,
sunglasses and visors are always a must.

We're the Merry Macs, we strive to cope
and pray that research will offer us hope
but we're still happy in spite of it all
as long as we don't stumble and fall.

With apologies to Cardinal Newman's Lead Kindly Light

THE BATHROOM NIGHT LIGHT

Lead kindly light,
lead thou me on
nocturnal visits
to the john.

Anabel LeFrancois

WHEN WILL I GROW UP?

At times
I get discouraged with the likes of me.
I make thoughtless mistakes,
lose my sense of timing,
say dumb things,
commit faux pas etc. etc.
As flawed human beings we should
strive to perfect ourselves,
then humbly accept imperfection.
It demands a lifelong struggle.
It's the endless paradox
and I may never feel grown up.

ON BEING UPTIGHT
ABOUT BEING RIGHT

Foresight and hindsight
span a mighty wide gap
with me in the middle
a-taking the rap
for
foresight is short sight
and who'll let me trade
two short sighted foresights
for a hindsight that's made?

Put another iron in the fire. Proverb.

PROBLEM SOLVING

This is the most challenging skill on the planet. Since we can't predict the future we evaluate and calculate, weigh, balance and counter- balance, pray and take action. That's the first iron put in the fire, plan 2 is another iron and plan 3, another.

In my mind's eye I see a blazing camp fire encircled with "problem solving" irons wearing little "hope caps".

This imaging makes me feel that with multiple solutions, and help from The Man Upstairs, the problem will eventually be resolved.

Life would be infinitely happier if we could only be born at the age of eighty and gradually approach eighteen.

-Mark Twain

Anabel LeFrancois

I GUESS IT'S
CALLED MATURITY

When I was young
I was very circumspect about me
and much too serious.
Now I view myself in funny cartoons.

When I was young
I carried the world on my shoulders,
wrote worried articles and poems
trying to make a difference.
My pen was not mightier than the sword.

When I was young
I thought the depression would never end,
then I thought the war would never end.
I thought the span of a long life
was an endless path.
Now I know better.

When I was young
much as I valued intelligence,
I yearned for the cookie cutter looks
of a movie star and didn't
appreciate my youthfulness.
Did any of us?

Me Too, My Friend

MY DAUGHTER'S PERSIAN CAT

My daughter has a Persian cat.
This cat adopted her.
Imploring eyes of emerald green
peered from a fluff of fur
as white as newly fallen snow.
Her monogram of black
graced ears and feet with flair and style
then with a practiced knack,
she curled her luscious tail,
meowed a coaxing plea.
All this she did with regal poise
and queenly dignity.
Though cats are not subservient
of that we're well aware,
they give one great companionship
so no one seems to care.
My daughter lost her heart that day,
She's mistress to a cat
who rules the roost with firm beguile
she has no quarrel with that.
They live in peaceful harmony;
both independent to the core
with give and take it seems to work,
they couldn't love each other more.
The fact remains...
her heart was hijacked by a cat.
My daughter buys her special food
she's likely to prefer
and pays the veterinary bills

Anabel LeFrancois

as incidents occur.
When she comes home she knows that she'll
be greeted at the door
with brushing up against her legs
and kitty cat rapport;
while dialoguing chatty purrs
she follows her about.
As roommates they're a happy pair;
there's not a shred of doubt.
We love cats cuddling on our laps
like stroking silky fur;
like listening to their motor hum,
enjoy their peaceful purr.
No creature is more beautiful,
more pleasing to the eye.
They are serene, they comfort us,
they're like a lullaby.
The fact remains;
her heart was hijacked by a cat.

Me Too, My Friend

VALUES

Our dog was a creature
whose outstanding feature
was a l-o-n-g- slimy tongue
that got me unstrung.
With too much emotion
she slathered her lotion;
I'd evade her affection
with instant rejection.

But then came a child
who didn't get riled,
bring things to a halt
like this squeamish adult.
She accepted the licking
and the love potion sticking
and after the pouncing
came proudly announcing,
"Duchess kissed me."

Anabel LeFrancois

THE BOTTOM LINE

At this point of my life
I exercise and walk our hills
with a brisk stride
because I want to avoid
the cane and walker.
I eat light and low fat
because I'm afraid
of heart attacks and strokes.
I drink the required water
because I don't want to dehydrate,
shrivel up and blow away.
I do all these things
because I see what happens
to people who don't.

I drink very little alcohol
because I'm a control freak.
I don't smoke because
I don't want to be bothered
with an oxygen tank
and tubes in my nose.
I don't do these things
because I see
what happens to people who do.

Me Too, My Friend

WHAT GOES AROUND
COMES AROUND

Remember when you were a child
and liked to play "go hide and seek?"
Seems now I'm playing it with things,
it's humbling and it makes me meek.

I play both roles, I hide, then seek,
an aggravating waste of time
when I should know, I put it there
no poltergeist, the blame is mine.

Inspired, I'll reorganize
and find a better, clever place.
I should record it on a card,
it could be lost without a trace.

WHY NOT?

You've been searching for hours,
you're quite drained and downcast.
There's a simple solution
look first where you look last.

Anabel LeFrancois

POWER STRIPES

They say polka dots symbolize power.
Says who? For whom? Women?
Polka dots are cowardly little balls
rolled up in the fetal position.
For me it's stripes,
stripes prevail in men's shirts.
They stand up straight
resolute
they make a statement,
that's power!

I buy shirts with vibrant stripes.
Their verticalness
makes me feel perky
and on some days,
like grandmother's corset
they fortify a wimpy spine.

Me Too, My Friend

REMEMBER WHEN

A scavenger hunt used to be fun?
Now it's called grocery shopping.
But where's the fun?
I've planned my menus for the week
and have a list of things I need;
the day that I find everything
will be a lucky day indeed.
I find the designated spots
too many choices of each brand
and scanning all that print's a chore,
we're folks who live in low fat land.
For special things I push the cart
from isle to isle, my steps retrace
remember where I found it last
they moved it to another place.
I heave a sigh and off I go
to find the next thing on the list
but it's too high for me to reach
I search for someone to assist.
I take a package in my hand
and through a magnifier squint
i'm hopeful for enlightenment
concerning each ingredient.
I'm ready for escape...
with most things in my cart I say,
"I'll find the rest another day."

Anabel LeFrancois

METHUSELAH MUSINGS

The Bible says that God worked for 6 days creating the earth and rested the seventh; in Genesis we read that a patriarch, Methuselah, lived to be 969 years old. This concept of time boggles the mind including their biological clocks but let's slip into fantasy. Methuselah, were you the one who said the first 100 years are the hardest? You had to wait until you were 187 years before you had your first son, then other sons and daughters followed. Were you a slow learner who had a century of fun trying? I envision your primitive life style and wonder how you endured the long centuries of being old with illness, ailments, aches, pains, depression, boredom with the repetitive mundane, teenagers taking too long to grow up, death of wives and peers, etc. etc. Methuselah, you were a good patriarch, why did God make you wait so long before taking you to your reward? I think you got a bum rap. I wouldn't want to hang around this planet as long as you had to. I hope you're happy now.

Me Too, My Friend

METHUSELAH

Do you recall, Methuselah
when you were white and old
a mild, a moonlit night
and a sweet vow you told?

Methuselah, do you recall
the song your heart had sung
when she was fair and love was all
and you were young?

Did you count the lonely century
and live the days again
when you were one hundred and twenty
and she, one hundred and ten?

-Leonard Feeney, S.J.

Note: Scientists have pinpointed the Methuselah gene, locating a stretch of DNA that confers healthy old age on men and women. The discovery unlocks the secret of long life. The studies took place in Iceland.

Anabel LeFrancois

A PHILOSOPHICAL
BIRTHDAY EPISTLE

A birthday comes, and 'custom' says
you have to count another year.
You're only one day older than
you were the day before, my dear.

You'll never be as young again
as you are on this very day.
Do not allow the count of years
to bother you or cause dismay.

So live today, you're young of heart,
let gayety reverberate.
The lucky day that you were born
is what we wish to celebrate.

DOES ANYBODY KNOW?

My neighbor was laboriously pulling the mixed variety of
early spring weeds in her front yard. As I passed by she com-
mented, "I've been wondering why the weeds are so much
smarter than my plants." Plants need TLC but, with no care,
weeds will grow in nooks and crannies, between cracks in
sidewalks and through asphalt. It's not fair.

Me Too, My Friend

MY THINK TANK,
THE DISH PAN

When I do dishes at the sink
I like to think!
As soapy water soaks the pans
and quickened hands
scurry to clear the cupboard top
in one nonstop transaction,
my mind takes fancy flights
to higher sights.
I escalate the stratosphere
with brain in gear.
Then I consider who I am
cleaning the jam...
solving the problems of the world
in apron clad.
My barnacles of wisdom fall
answers enthrall,
sparkling like cut glass in the suds.
Who are the duds
who run our land and make this mess?
I must confess
it's hard for me to comprehend
talents they spend to no avail
while things move toward
still more discord.
A dish pan's magic, you can see.
It can't be me.

RECOLLECTIONS

When I was a child, at family gatherings, I observed the old folks socializing with lively chatter and laughter and I'd think "How can they be so happy, soon they are going to die."

And now, here am I.

When I was a kid my grandmother's hands fascinated me and I, without prejudice, thought "Some day my hands will be like that from all the interesting things I'm going to do." My self fulfilling prophecy produced hands old before their time.

When I was in high school my friends and I fell into a stupid discussion guessing where each one of us would acquire their first wrinkles. Now we know.

When I was in my twenties my mother was fussing with the messiness of henna to cover the gray in her hair. I thought I'd never color my hair. I took a swatch of hair from my youth to a beautician and said "Match it."

THE SENIOR MOMENT CLUB

The word was here right on my tongue
it took to flight in outer space
can't finish what I had to say
a flustered look invades my face.

I scan the ceiling, there's no clue
it's playing cat and mouse with me.
When it's too late the teasing imp
comes back to me mischievously.

The fact remains
for someone else we're sharp as tacks.
At least we're not amnesiacs
not yet!

CANDLELIGHT

Candlelight
burns peeky holes
in the fabric of darkness
as we bask in the amber
eclipse of it's blush.

Anabel LeFrancois

ODE TO A MOUSE'S EAR

I tender salute
to all things minute...
the incredible smallness,
completeness, the all-ness
the crafted detail
exquisitely frail.

I find me enraptured
with the beauty that's captured
in this little cage.
T'would challenge a sage
to fathom the splendor
petiteness can render.
I think I'm astute
to tender salute.

When my son was in grade school we hosted the school hamster during Xmas vacation. Since the mouse was caged, I could enjoy it and I vowed that some day I would write an Ode to a Mouse's Ear.

Some day turned out to be decades later.

NOTHING

      is too small
           to be noticed
                to be explored
                    to be enjoyed.
                      NOTHING.

A VERY SMALL INCIDENT

My husband and I were grocery shopping and got momentarily separated. I looked around, approached a tall white haired man commenting on a produce. Flushed with embarrassment I sputtered, "Oh, I thought you were my husband." He looked me over from head to toe and with just a hint of a rakish grin said, "Maybe I should be."

I was too flustered to say Thank You and that man made my day.

Anabel LeFrancois

THE PERILS OF PAULINE

A chirping bird addressed the dawn
as she awakened with a yawn
luxuriating in her bed
until a thought popped in her head
that eggs and bacon would be great
to have upon her breakfast plate.

She fumbled taking out the eggs
they hit the floor, splashed on her legs.
She cleaned the mess, she'd start again
took out more eggs and guess what then,
her finger bumped a knife's sharp blade
the bacon fell and ricocheted.

Was this a dream or was it real?
She got things back on even keel,
the coffee burbled burblings
the bacon started sizzling
but while she watched the bacon most
to her disgust, she burned her toast.

At last she filled her breakfast plate
a meal no one could overrate.
To her chagrin and her surprise
it happened right before her eyes
while mastering her coffee mug
the bacon slid on braided rug.

Again she went on hands and knees
a feat she can't perform with ease.
She ate her eggs and toasted bread,
considered going back to bed,
fried bacon for herself instead.

A tribute to this legally blind friend.
With humor bubbling from within
she told this story with a grin.
She deals this way with everything;
I find her most inspiring.

TRIGGERINGS

It's fascinating sport to trace
the linkage of events
back to it's parent trigger.
Thought meanderings,
idle chatter
and the insignificant
can lead to who knows what?
Triggerings in retrospect
loom up as precious gifts
but who writes Thank You Notes
for triggerings?

Anabel LeFrancois

LET ME RUN AWAY

Written when I was seventeen

Let me run away with the wild spring wind a wind
that will do and dare,
let it slap my cheeks to a rosy red
and shoot pert fingers through my hair.

Let me run away with the wild spring wind
while it swirls in it's savage way,
let me skip and laugh and dance and sing
and go free with the wind today.

Written recently

Let me run and hide from the stinging wind
for the youthful thrill of it's romance died.
With my frozen feet and my fingers numb
I prefer the warmth of a fireside.

Me Too, My Friend

CONTINUED

I still laugh and dance and sing
but the wild spring wind is not my thing.
Its the beat of a forties big dance band
playing "In the Mood" that sends me.
The wildness of the wind invades me
as the beat goes on it's marathon...
The beat goes on
and I laugh and twirl
like a giddy girl.
Feet moving faster
flirt with disaster,
triple twirling
could send me a sprawling.
I'm really not cool
just a winded old fool.
The feet keep on moving
as though to be proving
for some silly reason
I can last through
the false endings teasing.
Somehow I knew it
I can still do it.

Anabel LeFrancois

MS. MIRACLE GROW

My friend delights in growing plants
and chronically fights bugs and ants.
she has a big variety
she nurtures with anxiety,
spends hours in the hot sun's glare
you've never seen such loving care,
and they reward her with their blooms
and their exotic, sweet perfumes.

And how much watering do you think
it takes to give them all a drink?
The time these plants monopolize
to cultivate and fertilize
with plants all over, high and low
in planters lined up in a row
like soldiers marching all around
her house and garden to astound,
give pleasure to the eye and soul.
It is indeed a worthy goal.

How many planters would you guess?
One hundred twenty six no less.

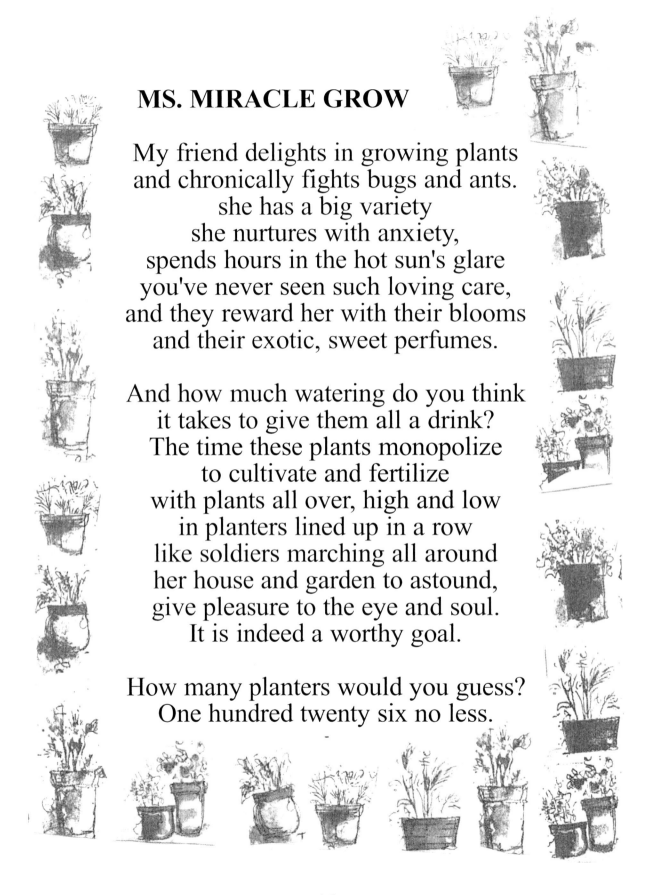

Me Too, My Friend

TRUE CONFESSIONS

That trusty short term memory
declines as we keep adding years.
There's humor in the mini-lapse
and we should share them with our peers.

A man I know told on himself
he had a nature call
while he was working in his yard.
It wasn't wise to stall
so back into the house he went
then stopped dead in his tracks.
What did he come back in to get?
Why was his brain so lax?

A lady started up the stairs
quite breathless stopped and with a frown,
she mused, what had she planned to get
and was she going up or down?

A man was being much maligned
by two old people full of wrath.
They both agreed this awful man
must surely be a psychopath.
There came an interrupting pause
and then one to the other said
"Who were we ranting on about?"
while scratching on his balding head.

47

Anabel LeFrancois

My letter writing friend put out
the mail and later in a daze
she picked it up delighted that
'twas personal, not throwaways.
Without her glasses and with haste
she opened up the mail she'd mailed.

Three cheers! We're laughing at ourselves,
much more, our humor has prevailed.

If you are ill, recovering from surgery or whatever....

GET WELL WISHES

Now this little ditty
may not be so witty
but simply addresses
itself to your stresses,
hope the treatment is working,
pain no longer lurking,
and you'll get better quicker
before you get sicker.

Me Too, My Friend

REMINISCING

I won't even tell my generation how old I was when I still believed in Santa. I ignored negative rumors at school because I was no dummy. As a responsible eldest of an expanding family I was convinced that my hard working parents' could never afford to buy those wonderful things we found under the tree on Xmas morning.

Like most children, we mailed our petitions to Santa. On Xmas Eve we put out cookies and milk for him which he ate, leaving a note saying that it was delicious and exactly what he needed to keep going. He also wrote each one of us a very personal, brief letter on the first page of a tablet he always left each one of us. We were special because no one we knew received letters from Santa. What's more, I never knew anyone else who mailed Santa Thank You letters after Xmas. As I write this I still remember how hard I worked trying to express my exuberant childish gratitude.

Anabel LeFrancois

MY FRIEND

She treads her days
with a gracious gentleness
speaking softly with kindliness.

She treads her days
with sensitive awareness
giving unselfishly.

She accepts
what cannot be changed
with serene resignation
and dignity.

She is a lady of quality
who has
fashioned herself
superbly.

Me Too, My Friend

THE ELUSIVE TRUTH

You won't get truth from politicians.
You won't find truth in advertising.
The printed word spawns propaganda
and bogus scams are truth disguising.
We search for truth in conversation,
find shreds of it in humorous joking.
For humans truth comes hard while
mirrors have honesty we find provoking.

SOMETHING TO THINK ABOUT

When I express an intuitive suspicion that there is a connection between impressionist art and macular degeneration I am politely rebuffed. That triggered a review of biographies. Cezanne and Monet were close in age and both suffered ridicule and poverty. In his youth Cezanne had an undiagnosed vision defect that prevented him from getting the result he so feverishly strived for. He enjoyed a brief period of limited acceptance before his death in 1906 at the age of 67. Monet changed his style in later years (a macular suspect) and died in 1924 at the age of 86. He was blessed with more good years of fame and financial reward. Beethoven composed music after he was deaf. For all of them it was genius that wouldn't give up. Bully for them.

Anabel LeFrancois

MARIN VALLEY'S PANORAMIC GIFT

Highway 101 splinters off to pursue
a road in these tree studded hills.
On reaching the summit you'll see
a breathtaking vista one eighty degrees
sprawling into the neighboring county.
San Pablo Bay in any mood, any season,
be it sunny, misty, hazy, or choppy,
or smooth as a mirror reflecting full moons,
never fails to seduce enchanted attention.
A clear day exposes a mystical view
of a myth-shrouded, remote Mt. Diablo.

A slow, leisured descent unravels new scenes
of primitive highland, habitat for the deer,
wild turkeys, raccoons, jack rabbits, and skunks,
occasional bob cats, possums and foxes,
many birds, hooting owls, cooing doves and
quail families who control moving traffic.

Keep going down further and further until
you're down looking up to a massive terrain
that stepladders into an azure blue sky.
Clouds billow themselves into whimsical shapes,
with serenity glide on their secret missions.

I've walked the contour of hills in the park,
even climbed to the rim and went hiking.
To capture the essence of this rustic beauty
in words is doomed to court failure. But I tried!

Me Too, My Friend

A HARD WORKING RETIREE

With a soul of a poet
and a vision in mind
he went out with a pickax
to the rim of our hills
to plant daffodil bulbs.
He delivered swift blows
to the hard crusted sod.
Though ax handles were broken,
the bulbs got positioned
in tiny earth pockets
and given strict orders
to do what all good bulbs do.
He came down to the Clubhouse,
then tackled the sides of the road
and he kept right on digging
and digging and digging
until five hundred bulbs
had cozy earth pockets.

The Marin Valley people
look on with amazement
at bright yellow patches
accenting the lush greenery of spring.
Poets write of daffodils,
but this man makes them happen.

Anabel LeFrancois

THINGS THAT MAKE MY DAY

It tingles me
when humor makes pings
at the folly of things.
    It tickles me
    to witness a grin
    that shouldn't have been.
It busies me
to riddle the why's
of foibles disguise
    It livens me
    to see third eye slants
    bedeviling the cants.
It touches me
to see the warmth of a heart
crafting it's art.
    It pleases me
    to see joy reach it's goal
    in the eye of the soul.
It gladdens me
to see splinters of God
in things that are odd.

Me Too, My Friend

THE BRIDESMAID

She stood tall and slim and poised
with a regal, unaffected grace
as she walked down the isle.

Brunette beauty
flattered pale chiffon,
large excited eyes
overcasted awed solemnity.
Flushed cheeks and lips accented
her lovely uncosmeticed face.
Slender fingers encircled
the pristine modesty of daisies
that merged with the innocence
of sweet sixteen.
A portrait of pure naturalness.
Oh what a sight was she!

Word pictures fail,
the camera fails,
and how could the spell of the moment
be suspended in a pose for canvass
or for a Grecian urn?
Is this why mothers cry at weddings?

Anabel LeFrancois

THE QUAIL FAMILY

We live in the country
away from the crowds,
where the quail reside.
We're lucky!
These adorable creatures enthrall,
capture hearts with their blatant petite-ness.
Small feathery balls hurry and scurry
on thin wire legs roller blading,
little bobbing heads hastily pecking at seeds,
mama, absorbed in nurturing,
papa, enthroned on a fence post,
protecting with squawking authority.
A minor disturbance triggers
a flurry of skitter and scatter,
fragile survival in constant threat.
Quail families and tiny quail babies
so fascinating to watch from nesting,
hatching to maturing
delight, give pleasure,
enrich our lives.
Their survival prompts country roads
to sprout signs warning cars to slow down.
Quail have the Right of Way.

Me Too, My Friend

THE APPLE

The old theory that the apple doesn't fall far from the tree has been proven again by my son and his offspring in fourth grade school essays entitled:

WHY I WOULD, OR WOULD NOT GO ON THE VOYAGE WITH COLUMBUS

If I were alive when Columbus was I probably would not go with Columbus on his first voyage across the ocean. I wouldn't have gone on the first voyage because I'd probably have a job and I wouldn't want to leave it. I would probably believe the world is flat like the rest of the people. I might not like Columbus and I wouldn't want to hang around him. I might be a man who gets sea sick when he goes out to sea. The men on the crew were released from jail to go on the voyage and I might not want to go on the voyage because of them. Those are my reasons for not going.

He is now a pilot and F.A.A. Satety Inspector.

Anabel LeFrancois

Essay of his offspring:

Don't want to go because of all problems explorers like Columbus had. Their slaves died of hunger, didn't have enough space. The voyage lasted too long, there were no rest rooms, the food had germs in it and did not taste good. Those are some of the reasons why I do not want to go. Another reason is that it would be boring and I would get sea sick; also, our ship might be taken over by pirates and we might get shot at.

Another essay

WOULD YOU LIKE TO BE AN EXPLORER?

I think to be an explorer would be exciting but after a while it would be boring. I would be a great captain. I would not boss my crew around. Storms would come, maybe even hurricanes. On a second thought I don't want to be an explorer because it's way too dangerous. It might be fun though and after I came back I would be famous.

Me Too, My Friend

HAPPY BIRTHDAY
and
This is why there aren't more
candles on your birthday cake

How many people would it take
to light up candles on your cake?

And then how many labored blows
t'would take to put them out? Who knows?

The wish you made would not come true
so let's not make that big snafu.

Plus no one likes the melted wax
that on the icing drips and stacks.

Who wants to watch you huff and puff,
you wouldn't do it fast enough.

So let's cut out the protocol
and start to serve the alcohol

for drinking toasts is much more fun
and eating cake suits everyone.

Anabel LeFrancois

WHAT IF?

If I get overly impressed
with my antiquity
and put myself upon the shelf,
become an absentee

t'would be a big mistake I think,
for motivation dies
when throttled with reclusiveness
and severance of ties.

What if I live a hundred years?
T'would be an awful shame
I'd think about the wasted years
and just have me to blame.

Me Too, My Friend

SHE LIVED TO BE ONE HUNDRED

Hurrah and three cheers
for the century of years
that this lady's been given.
Through sunshine and storm
she's loving and warm
as she goes through the business of living.
She moved to our park
brought spirit and spark
got active and worked in the kitchen.
Invented "I Care"
and emceed with a flair
hat shows that were downright bewitch'in.

And that isn't all
The Whistlestop call
she answered and years found her sewing
lap quilts by the score
and things needed for
the ill and her work crew kept growing.
Her memory can scan
a century's span
the earthquake of 06,
the women's suppression
world wars one and two
the science breakthrough
disasters, good times and all the depressions.

Anabel LeFrancois

So let us give thanks
she's tops in the ranks
of souls that have tried and arriv'in.
Hurrah and three cheers
She outlived her peers,
survived one hundred years.

WISDOM

When I have ceased to break my wings
against the faultiness of things
and learn that compromises wait
behind each partly opened gate,
when I can look LIFE in the eyes
grown calm and very coldly wise,
life will have given me the Truth
and taken in exchange, my Youth.

Sara Teasdale

Me Too, My Friend

MY HOBBY

A train of thoughts rumble through my mind,
ideas revolve on a merry go-round
grasping for attention and expression
that sparkles with fresh originality.
Normal activities are punctured by invading
word substitutions, phrase substitutions.
Words, words, words kaleidoscope in my head
shaping themselves into different patterns
over and over and over again until
final choices are made and I succeed or fail.
I say it's playing with my head
and call this agonizing chore a hobby.
The inspiration to write about the mundane
with limited skill mystifies me
but the urge challenges, overpowers.
I'm not complaining,
only viewing my idiosyncrasy
with self-deprecating amusement.
At best this "brain strain"
should forestall dementia.

Anabel LeFrancois

THAT WAS THEN, THIS IS NOW

(Expressing thoughts of a friend
anticipating life in a Retirement Home.)

When I was young, I liked to cook.

On looking back I calculate
those fifty thousand meals we ate

prepared by me, without a doubt
has left me totally burned out.

My kitchen could be "state of art"
now cooking's not what I'm about.

Retirement is here at last
they say their chef is unsurpassed.

I'll now be served and dine in style
devote my time to things worthwhile.

With liberation from the kitchen
I'll live my life without restriction.

Me Too, My Friend

MY TOTEM POLE

This totem pole is
a custom made symbol
of primitive ME.
It's shocking to observe
this stiff structure
that human frailty
and immaturity
has clumsily carved
but there it is...
my edifice of past errors
blunders and stupidities
disappointments in self,
inane face upon face
staring hard
into the reality
of the present.

The mentality of maturity
looks back through
the tunnel of time
with limited memory
and judges harshly.
Guilt stings.

Anabel LeFrancois

MAKING SENSE OF FAILURES

We all have mocking
totem poles to haunt us.
We enter the realm of
consciousness as neophytes
starting with a blank.
Wisdom is bought with pain
and self effacing insight.
To live is to make mistakes.
It's called experience and it
happens when we risk failure
to take chances.
Mistakes are miscalculations
by which we learn.
In all honesty, could hoarding
grief over past decisions
gone wrong be coddling
wounded pride?
We should give ourselves
permission to be imperfect,
give others permission
and forgive all.
It makes no sense to beat
ourselves up. We carry on.
Totem poles teach humility.

Me Too, My Friend

AN UNFORGETABLE MAN

Lew was a good person who viewed everyone as a friend. He had a ready smile, a hearty laugh and a handshake oblivious of it's strength. He was a happy free spirit who gratefully greeted each new day with a bicycle ride to a donut shop and chatter with the regulars. He had his plans for the day and something of interest for a story always happened.

During World War II, his adventures as a merchant marine gave him a lifetime supply of stories to tell. After the war he went to work at San Quentin Prison as a correction officer, giving him fuel for more stories to relate, including being involved and testifying in the famous Jackson Five shoot out. He spoke to the younger prisoners about motorcycles, fishing and sports as he skillfully climbed ladders and slithered up and down poles. He gave them respectful recognition and positive support. He married, had five children; widowed when the youngest was nine.

In 1980 we met Lew who enlivened our social life with his contagiously chronic good mood and his flair for having fun. As a severely addicted punster he took razzing that only encouraged him. As a singer he was an eager performer. As a ballroom dancer he was a natural and he cut a dashing figure in his tuxedo. In an old pickup truck he courted and won the heart of an elegant retired ballerina. They laughed, danced and twirled through many evenings in ballrooms and on cruises attracting admiring attention.

Anabel LeFrancois

Gift making was always a work in progress and he had a talent for carving and whittling wood into whales, dolphins and fish. For children he made sail boats and with pine cones he invented Whahoo birds complete with a story about them. The many clever things he came up with was limitless.

Retirement years were spent working on a vintage classic Jaguar that rarely ran and a 35 ft. sail boat that rarely sailed. Ever optimistic of his mechanical skills, he resisted discouragement and thoroughly enjoyed all the action on the dock. When he wanted to be on the water he got out his canoe and paddled for miles. Adapt with hammer and saw, he was a Mr. Fix It who would tackle anything and everything. He made effective fishing lures out of discarded teaspoons and bullet casings from the firing range.

Lew was a rugged, strong muscled man to the end. His favorite toast was "Health is Wealth." If he was sick he wouldn't know it. In his seventies he bicycled 500 miles to attend his niece's wedding in LA. A fifty mile detour did not phase him. He lost a car at the Oakland Airport; spending all day looking for it in vain, he took a bus back to San Rafael returning the next day. That nightmare turned into a funny story including how things had changed, again slipping into his role as verbal historian of the Bay Area.

He rode his motorcycle all over the surrounding counties, making countless trips to the Northwest. One cold night in Montana upon investigating motel rates he said "I didn't say I wanted to buy your motel, I just want to spend one night in it."

Me Too, My Friend

He camped outside and wound up in the hospital. After a long recovery from a motorcycle accident in '99 he was again out on the highways.

Lew was not one to mourn failures. The fact that the boat didn't sail and the Jaguar didn't run mattered not. With resignation he was happy doing what he was doing. He was at peace with himself and the world. He was a man of integrity, true to himself and true to all who knew him. Though he had an identical twin brother he was like no other.

On his way to visit a son in Seattle an accident proved fatal. The police never heard of an 85 year old man even riding on a motorcycle and the hospital couldn't believe his age. Frugal with self, always ready to lend a helpful hand to others, relaxed and forgetful, he lived in the moment. No narrow grave for Lew, his ashes went under the Golden Gate Bridge to the freedom of the sea.

EVERYBODY HAS THEIR STORY

I'm looking across a crowded room of a senior gathering. Defective hearing escalates the noise level as they good naturedly attempt to communicate with each other. I think of all those individual lives, each unique, lived in different circumstances, facing all sorts of difficulties and challenges, regretting that too many of those wonderful, "stranger than fiction" stories will never be told.

Anabel LeFrancois

METAMORPHOSIS

When the essence of my soul has flown the limits of some outer space the earthbound shell of flesh and bone shuns rest in peace, slow metamorphosis within the claustrophobic grave gouged in the earth or silence chilled in Mausoleum walls. Cremation's instant ash gives freedom to wide expanse of earth and sky, bird song and noises of things living. Let ashes of old flesh and bone be flown into the clouds and left to parachute into the arms of forest trees, enjoy their lingering embrace until capricious elements decree another residence. Old flesh and bones are vagabonds exploring and recycling in other forms of life seeking redemption in some divine equation. That part of me that is the promised immortality of soul lives on in some mysterious celestial realm of God's infinity. I am the essence of "to be."

Me Too, My Friend

A GOOD THING TO FORGET

I visited a neighbor and discovered that, though in need of knee surgery, she had painted her kitchen and living room. Since she could only tolerate standing a short period of time, I was awe stricken. What patience that must have taken. As I was leaving she mentioned her intention to do some wall papering and I was quick to volunteer my help. She said "I've done a lot of wall papering and I'm only doing a small area." I did a double take and said "It's a good thing, I forgot I can't see." She laughed and said "I forget I can't walk." That's a good thing. We don't limit ourselves.

AFTER-THOUGHTS

Every day I thank God that I can swing my arms and walk fast with limber ease and enjoyment. No doubt she thanks God every day that she can see. Mary Tyler Moore once said in an interview that no one on this planet escapes without having to deal with some-thing. My grandmother said that if we all put our personal crosses on a heap and given the freedom to choose a different one, we'd probably choose our own familiar cross.

Anabel LeFrancois

FOR SALE

The sewing machine has
permanent residence in the closet,
it's owner's blind
beyond all needle threaders.

Seventy years of sewing history
exhausted two machines.
The third one, almost new,
needs someone else
to thread it's needle
and delight in creating things
unique and beautiful
one does not see in stores.

Pervasive thoughts persist,
"It's time to let it go."

OVERHEARD

At a festive event, my friend, upon being complimented on her attire
replied with a simple "Thank You" and "I've enjoyed it for many
years."

Me Too, My Friend

TODAY I PLAYED CARPENTER

Perhaps for the last time.
Measured inches through a magnifying glass.
The saber saw seemed heavier
and the brads almost invisible.
With focusing dysfunctional
and depth perception nil,
struggled on by trial and error.
Eventually the job was finished
without too many hammer "ouches";
fixall, sanding and paint
will make the job passable.

Wood scraps enhance a storage cube
and rescued it from stark nakedness.
Tonight I'll go to bed
grateful that I succeeded one more time.
These minor carpentry endeavors
should be brought to a halt
but
the challenge is seductive,
only failures
will extinguish the fueled determination
of a life-long compulsive
do-it-your-selfer.

Anabel LeFrancois

DISCIPLINE

Our need of it has no let up.
A harsh Master, it lays a heavy hand
on our shoulders
from toddler training to the grave.
Through disappointments and heartache
we finally learn that control outside of
ourselves has limitations.

When things went wrong
screws tightened down upon us,
it was a "call to arms"
we squared our shoulders
and we coped as best we could.

It's true in leisure years,
some disciplines can be relaxed,
but all too soon those few golden years
of freedom and exploration are
interrupted with menacing health
problems bringing with them demands
for unrelenting self discipline.
We've been in training all our lives.
What else is new?

Note: The transition to this advance stage of mascular degeneration was mercifully slow, a snail's pace, metering time over a period of fifteen years. Like the snail, resignation also takes it's time.

Me Too, My Friend

MAKING ADJUSTMENTS

Sunlight betrays,
blinding glare shrinks
into shadows and darkness
my step falters.

Lighting conditions
command faces
to blur into blanks
like Amish dolls.

Eye contact is lost.
Not seeing eyes
those "windows of the soul"
is a sad privation.

I must hone other skills
to compensate.
Others do it, so can I.

Now that "seductive challenge"
that fueled my determination
to accomplish other things
must turn to developing coping skills
of an ever increasing higher caliber.

Anabel LeFrancois

HAPPY HEAD

I have a happy head.
It spawns a swarming
bee hive of ideas for:
the well turned phrase, the rhythmic rhyme
problem solving action plans and schemes
creative projects of any description
overly ambitious artistic endeavors.

I fall in love with many of these ideas,
motivation jet propels action and a chain
reaction is set in motion
until a satisfactory completion happens.

According to the experts that's O.K.
This merry-go-round of activities and goals
minimizes time spent with worry beads
that go from hand to pocket.

This busy-head syndrome I've concluded,
like macular degeneration, is part of my
inheritance.

Me Too, My Friend

This Cartoon was given to me by a neighbor who follows the progress of my projects with avid interest.

"Wherever I go, I have an urgent need to redecorate. Is that a sin, Father?

When my daughter calls me her salutation is an amused, bouncy question "What are you doing Mother?"

77

Anabel LeFrancois

A PRAYER

Give me the serenity
to accept what cannot be changed
with courage and patience.

Help me to avoid being
more dependent than necessary,
to exert all my God given talent
to sharpen and improve
coping skills.

Help me to guard against stubbornness
to relinquish activities
that put me in danger
or place a burden on others.

Give me the wisdom
to know one from the other.

Me Too, My Friend

SAYISMS, My favorites:

When life gives you lemons make lemonade.

OH God! make bad people good and make good people nice.

Choose your thoughts as you would a bouquet.

She didn't know it couldn't be done so she did it.

There is a way of listening that surpasses all compliments.

Getting old isn't so bad when you consider the alternative.

Youth is a thing of beauty,
Age is a work of art.

Worry is today's mouse eating yesterday's cheese.

Adults are desensitized children.

It's never too late to have a happy childhood.

Emotions have no I.Q. and no reality.
Emotions only have feelings to be dealt with.

Each night God gives us a sunset for sleep
and rest to separate us from tomorrow's problems.

How old would you be if you didn't know how old you was?

Anabel LeFrancois

When you think of your loved ones who have
gone to their reward you have one foot in
Heaven. Me

Faith in Hope is a virtue.
To Hope for Faith is a prayer. Me

An Idea is the most exciting thing in the world because it is
the seed that grows into happenings. Me

FAVORITE QUOTES

I am part of all that I have met.

Tennyson

If eyes were made for seeing then beauty is it's own excuse
for being.

Ralph Waldo Emerson

It matters not how strait the gate
how charged with punishment the scroll,
I am the Master of my fate
I am the Captain of my soul.

From Invictus by William Henley

Me Too, My Friend

INCORRIGIBIE

I carry my optimism like a little
girl
with a balloon on a stick.
Everyone knows balloons
bouncing
on sticks above heads of
tripping little girls
are vulnerable
but
balloons are easy to come by
and there's something to be said
for fresh air in new balloons
so why should I change?

FAITH IN HOPE

If popped balloons
exhale stale dreams
that lay shriveled at my feet,
the grieving shall be brief.
When I am tired of the pain
once again
I will pump freshness
from virgin depths within me
into thin structured
walls of hope.

Anabel LeFrancois

THE WISHING WELL

I wish for you a heart that sings
gay songs that glide on bluebird wings
dispersing happiness and joy
with self's melodious decoy,

a mind that probes and contemplates
the other side of Heaven's gates
to learn the mysteries of God
while feet of clay are plodding sod.

I wish for you beauty of thought
and wisdom that white truth has bought,
contentment and a peace of mind
in harmony with all you find.

For you I want no compromise,
Heaven on earth, then Paradise.

Me Too, My Friend

PRAYER OF ST. FRANCIS OF ASSISI

Lord make me an instrument of your peace.
Where there is hatred, let me sow love,
Where there is injury, pardon,
Where there is doubt, faith,
Where there is despair, hope,
Where there is darkness, light
and where there is sadness, joy...

Oh Divine Master, grant that I may not
so much seek to be consoled as to console;

To be understood as to understand;
To be loved as to love;

For it is in giving that we receive;
It is in pardoning that we are pardoned;

and it is in dying that we are born to eternal life.

Anabel LeFrancois

EPILOGUE

After this book was written, I had a dream in which my vision suddenly returned to normal. I could see things in detail, colors were vivid and beautiful. I went about exploring things with great enjoyment. My emotions were so over-whelming that I felt the urge to weep with joy but I was engaged in conversation with a lady and controlled myself. All of a sudden I could not hear what her moving lips were saying. The loss of the sense of hearing was dismissed as "mute on the remote control." Then I awakened in a state of awe and luxuriated in the good feeling it left with me. I didn't want to speak or break the spell. It was so real that a thought surfaced, what if....the incorrigible little girl running with a balloon on a stick, looked into the mirror and saw a blur of hair and a featureless face. But the good feeling persisted. A popped balloon didn't seem to puncture the euphoria. The dream spoke it's message. Status quo was reinstated, I had plans for the new day that was glistening in the freshness of morning.

Epilogue…..Seize the moment

Six months later, as we drive flat, arid country in Washington state, the black ribbon of asphalt in front of us contrasts against a pale blue horizon. To the amazement of this sky worshipper, all cumulus clouds deserted the dome of the sky, hugged the ground and formed a solid wall of uniform height that encircled and pro-tectively enveloped us. A most unusual sight to be captured on canvas but what artist would dare face the rebuff of unbelieving critics? This is reality in its most incredible form and I am witness to the truth.

The somber monotone shoulder of the road blurs into invisibility and seems to fade into the atmosphere creating a momentary sensation of a humble Toyota, defying gravity, sky riding up hill on a black ribbon. This is not reality! I know my eyes are lying! I choose to treasure the illusion and consider it a secret revelation, like filigreed headlight halos adorning dark freeways with special lighting affects meant to be seen only by people with defective vision.

Epilogue.…...Faith in hope pays off

Two weeks later when this book was about to go to print my Ophthalmologist announced that since I had little to lose he would perform cataract surgery. I was enthusiastic and hopeful. The surgery went well, and I am experiencing an exciting recovery. It is now day seven after surgery and each day I am noticing gradual improvement in my vision. I have been rescued from the fog that enveloped me, the extreme sensitivity to glare has vanished and I am thrilled to see vibrant colors, definition of form and some texture in all things from my home surroundings to all of nature. I can cope with blind spots and other limitations. Peripheral vision should not be underrated; therapy can teach more efficient usage. I share this with you because I wish to leave you with hope. Research has identified the macular gene. There is reason for optimism. Instead of leaving you as one going into a denser fog, I am going into a cheerful, brighter world. My dream described in the beginning of this epilogue has partially come true. Whatever the problem, medical or personal, try to have faith and Hope.

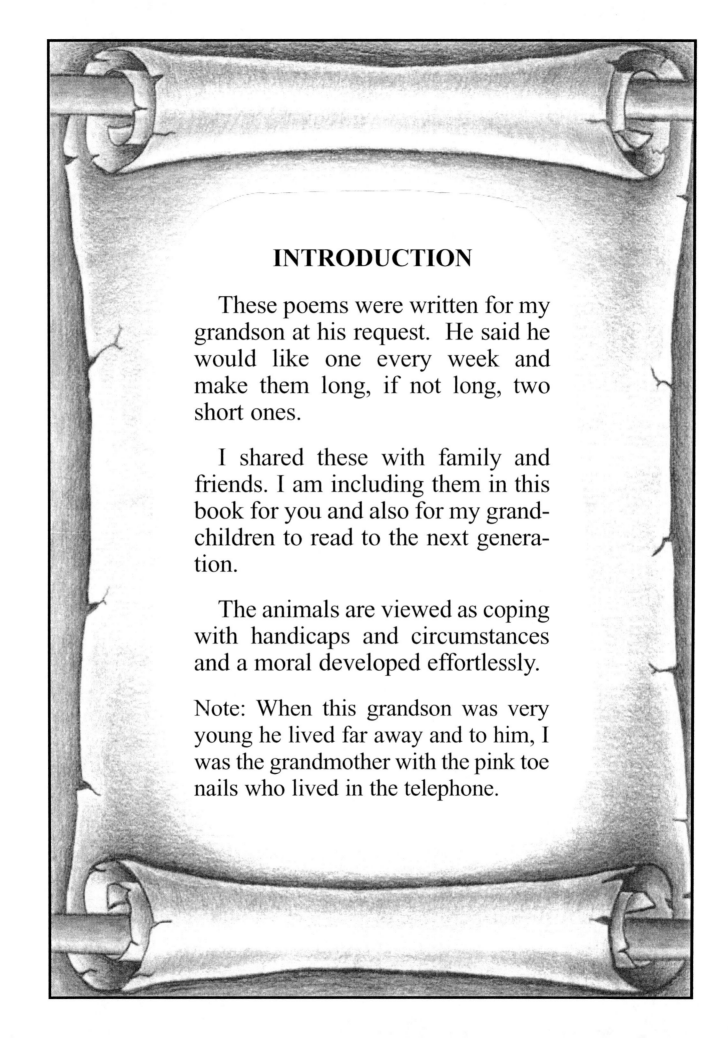

INTRODUCTION

These poems were written for my grandson at his request. He said he would like one every week and make them long, if not long, two short ones.

I shared these with family and friends. I am including them in this book for you and also for my grandchildren to read to the next generation.

The animals are viewed as coping with handicaps and circumstances and a moral developed effortlessly.

Note: When this grandson was very young he lived far away and to him, I was the grandmother with the pink toe nails who lived in the telephone.

Anabel LeFrancois

A FANTASY TRIP

Wrap me in a rainbow
take me to the moon
let me gather gold dust
where the stars are strewn.
Oh! to reach the dipper
steal a giddy ride
down it's lengthy handle
tumbling inside,
do some twirls and dancing
climbing to the rim,
checking the horizon
acting on a whim,
joyride on a rocket
weightless in the air
whirling round the planets
flying everywhere.
When the day is dawning
fluffy clouds appear
singing angels at their harps
charm the atmosphere.
Think that Grandma's lost it?
Take a hint from me,
never lose that playful
love of fantasy.

Me Too, My Friend

EASTER EGG HUNT

Happy Easter to C.J.
on this special day
when he runs on little legs
hunting pretty Easter eggs
painted up in multi colors
of the rainbow and he hollers
laughs and giggles with delight
opens mouth and takes a bite
of a chocolate bunny's ear.
Then he gets his legs in gear
and runs off in search of more.
He is having fun galore
finding eggs to fill his basket
but he sometimes hurries past it
where another finds it hidden,
C.J. takes a little kidding
then goes on his merry chase
till he covers every base.

Easter's fun and that's for sure
worth what older folks endure
to see children laugh and play.
If it's wet and windy out
hunting takes a different route.

Upstairs, downstairs, nooks and crannies
running off their little fannies

Anabel LeFrancois

till the house is one disaster
nothing makes it happen faster
than a wintry Easter morn
when outside's a blustery storm.

Makes no difference, Easter's fun
whether it be rain or sun.
Happy Easter dear C.J.
on this very special day.

A CHILD'S WISH

I wish I was a little boy
who played when Jesus played
I'd give him one of my best toys
for one that Joseph made.

Note: This was written by one
of my school mates.

Me Too, My Friend

WHY DO TOES WRINKLE IN THE TUB?

Rub a-dub dub
C.J.'s in the tub
his toes are all wrinkled
his fingers are crinkled.
He wants to know why
and wonders if I
have an answer for him.

Not to worry, they won't shrivel
fall off your hands and feet
A long time you've been soaking
in your soapy bubble treat.

It's a fact, skin on your fingers
and the skin that's on your toes
is quite thick, acts like a blotter
that is where the water goes.

All your spongy pores it's filling,
till there's no more room to be,
so your skin begins to crinkle
while you splashed and laughed with glee.

Later on you're bound to notice
when you're working hard at play
toes and fingers will look normal.
All your wrinkles went away.

Anabel LeFrancois

DO CATS HAVE BELLY BUTTONS?

I will tell you where they're at.
A belly button on a cat
isn't easy to be found.
You will have to look around
furry areas real slow
several inches and below
kitty's rib cage there's a scar.
That is where the buttons are,
oval shaped, so very small
they are hardly seen at all.

Belly buttons, hardly real,
on a cat they're no big deal.

Me Too, My Friend

THE CUTE STINKY SKUNK

Now a skunk is clever
and a skunk is cute
and he has a weapon
you can't dispute
that a thing so smelly,
so stinky so strong
it seems unlikely
it could belong
to this cute thing
with fur so sleek
so black and pretty
with it's white streak
a tail so graceful
you want to pet
this cute kitty
but you would get a
spray of "pew"
so very fast
you'd hold your nose,
it's meant to last
a long, long time

and you would be
in isolation
undoubtedly.
Though the skunk is small
he's bound to win
in any scuffle
he might get in.

Anabel LeFrancois

MONKEYS

Have you ever wondered why it's so much fun to watch the monkeys at the zoo? And did you ever figure out that's it's because of all the creatures in this world the monkeys most resemble you? They use their agile arms and legs like you when hanging on the playground bars. They like to swing and jump around and love to mimic anyone who comes within their view. They play the clown to make you laugh and if you clap they'll clap right back, they'll rub their ears, make monkeyshines. Now all these things are also things you think it's fun to do. To be the center of attention you'll giggle, laugh and play the clown. It fills your little heart with glee to make a body laugh. The antics of the monkey tickle you. You tickle him that's why he mimics you.

THE THREE LEGGED CAT

Today I encountered a three legged cat
who obviously can't catch a four legged rat
or rapturously snatch a two legged bird.
Meeoows at back doors were obviously heard
In somebody's home he's a permanent guest
He hobbles along and then takes a rest.
I admire this cat who can't catch a rat.
On a second thought, maybe he can.

Me Too, My Friend

DO GOATS REALLY EAT TIN CANS?

Eating cans is a fable
but they relish the label.
Unlike me and you
they like to eat glue,
the reason is his
bacteria is
a thing in his gut,
a fabulous "what"
enabling him
to pamper his whim
for paper and glue
without any harm
or stomach alarm.

The diet of goats
according to quotes
is incredibly strange
takes in a wide range.

They're human lawn mowers
and handy leaf blowers.

Anabel LeFrancois

THE TURTLE

The turtle is clever, as clever can be
because he's equipped so efficiently
to take his house with him wherever he goes
convenient for him as everyone knows.

There's no doubt about it, the turtle is blest
whenever he's tired and yearns for a rest
he pulls in his legs and retracts his head,
his shell is a canopy over his bed.

He snoozes a while, then goes on his way.
How lucky for him with no rent to pay.
When God made the turtle so very unique
so patient, so mild, so gentle, so meek,

He built in a message quite rigid and stern
the turtle must "move it" when food's a concern.
Survival demands he come out of his shell
that must be the lesson the turtle can tell.

Here's what it's about....
Just stick your neck out.

Me Too, My Friend

A LOVE AFFAIR

I have a little friend
who thinks the living end
is a horse.

Her name is Debbie Coots
and I think she's in cahoots
with a horse.

Now her horse's name is Joker
and if you much as poke her
she will gallop.

She's a dilly of a filly
and she takes the country hilly
it's a wallop.

Galloping, frolicking,
galloping, rollicking
airily, merrily.
rollicking.

Little Debbie courts disaster
always wanting to go faster
than she should,

and there's nothing she likes better
than to feed her and to pet her

Anabel LeFrancois

it's because
with rapport and understanding
horsy love keeps on expanding
they are friends.

I don't know a happier girlie
who gets up so bright and early
just to go

Galloping, frolicking,
galloping, rollicking
airily, merrily.
rollicking.

her whole life's a joyful tizzy
with a horse to keep her busy
for she's "hitched"
to her horse.

Galloping, frolicking,
galloping, rollicking
airily, merrily.
rollicking.

Me Too, My Friend

A TRUE BEDTIME STORY

There were identical twins named Sparkle and Glisten. It may surprise you to know that they were a pair of earrings. They were the happiest when they were in a jewelry box because then they could be together and have fun sharing things, laugh and giggle. When the grandmother took them out, she put one on each ear and they were separated but they knew it would not be for long and they would be back together again in the jewelry box sharing what they saw and heard on outings. Life was interesting and fun because the grandmother only took Sparkle and Glitter out when she was attending something very special, like weddings, balls, birthday parties and cruises. One time things went very wrong and Sparkle found herself slipping. She hung on for dear life but she lost her grip and took a fall. She wound up on the car seat on a sweater and when that was picked up, she fell to the floor and then got kicked by the toe of a shoe winding up in dust under the front car seat. She was terrified! No one would ever find her and what would she do without Glisten? When the grandmother got home, she had no earrings to put in the jewelry box. Sparkle was so lonely and thought of Glitter alone in the jewelry box wondering what had happened to her. It was unbearable. Days dragged into weeks and weeks into months and the lady who owned the car decided to clean her car inside and out. She pulled a cleaning rag out from under the car seat and lo and behold, Sparkle came tumbling out and skittered on the floor. The lady let out a big "Oh" and put Sparkle in her pocket; then she removed the carpet and shook it out over the

Anabel LeFrancois

flower bed by the car port. Sparkle was so excited and happy but when she was put in the jewelry box, she found herself all alone. Glitter was not there and though she was in a better place, she was heartbroken. Days dragged on into weeks and weeks into months and spring came. The lady decided to work up the soil in the flower bed by the carport and you won't believe what she found in the dirt. Can you make a guess? There was Glitter, dull and tarnished. She had been buried all those months in the dirt and her misery must have been incredible. Can you imagine how happy Sparkle and Glitter were to be back together again? The grandmother was happy, the lady who found the earrings was happy and I'm sure you are happy because we all like stories with happy endings. This really happened and the grandmother and the lady asked me to tell their unusual story about the lost and found earrings.

THE PELICAN

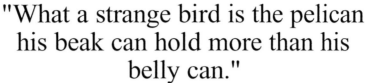

"What a strange bird is the pelican
his beak can hold more than his
belly can."
Grandma is sorry she cannot take credit
for saying those witty words.
Ogden Nash was the poet who said it
about those incredible birds.
The poor pelican has a pinched vertebrae
in his neck and he isn't able
to raise up his head and that isn't all
it's his beak that gave him a label.
For the pelican's in a class by himself
and his beak gets all the attention.
It's a foot in length and six inches in depth,
a ridiculous, clumsy extension,
an unfortunate circumstance to be sure
but the bird would not be outwitted.
With a tweak and a nudge, says he to himself,
"I'm blest, in fact I'm outfitted
with a wonderful net for scooping up fish,
for the young it's a marvelous feeding dish."
If a bird brain can come up with something that good
it behooves us to ponder and see if we could;
for life is a series of problems evolving
there's never a shortage of things that
need solving.

Anabel LeFrancois

IS THE OWL REALLY WISE?

Is the owl really wise
or did folklore devise
a story to tell
and magic to sell?
Who connected the owl,
such a nocturnal fowl,
to learning and books
and scholarly looks?

T'was the custom, the norm,
that the bell handle form
be shaped like the bird
and rung to be heard
by students in school,
t'was the teachers best tool
and worked out just fine
to keep kids in line.

Does it make any sense
and what's the defense
of making kids rise
with sleep in their eyes
when the owl's in a tree
resting up from a spree?

He caroused through the night
till dawn's early light.

Me Too, My Friend

How about all that stuff
they dish out so tough,
"Arise with the sun and get your work done?"

Lots of credit owls got
and example they're not.
The kids do not buy
this obvious lie.
On a scale one to ten
the bird's never been,
without being biased
I'd say he's been minus-ed.

Note: In Greece all the bell handles we saw were in the shape of an owl, even the large ones.

Anabel LeFrancois

FLYING HIGH

Like the roar of a tiger the big engines throb
all ready to take off and puncture the sky.
With it's nose pointed upward it lifts off the ground
and makes like an eagle until it's so high

it is piercing the sky and you're flying above
the fluffy white clouds like a carpet of snow
and it looks like it's safe, you imagine you could
go walking or running and not fall below.

It deceptively looks like a great place to ski
whenever you'd fall a soft cloud would be there
to absorb and to cushion, you'd never get hurt
with reckless abandon you'd ski through the air.

I suggest that you look at the dome of the sky
assuming that heaven is not very far
that angels have slipped through the white pearly gates
to serenade earthlings or swing on a star.

It's pretty and peaceful surrounded by blue
with silver and white fleecy clouds for a floor
you're higher than eagles and closer to God
adventuring space as higher you soar.

The breath-taking beauty of nature expands
you're flying and seeing the world from afar.
As you start your descent and you come close to earth
your ears may be popping, air pockets may jar

Me Too, My Friend

but the sights you will see will distract you I'm sure
the mountains are mole hills and everything seems
to be miniature, tiny the bushes and trees,
the rivers, the lakes, meandering streams.

All the countryside looks like a colorful quilt
the fields are like patches, all different in shape
ever changing and pretty, an artist could search
forever not finding a better landscape.

Now the scene keeps on changing as lower you go
and things all look small just like pocket sized toys,
city blocks with houses and yards that are fenced,
the freeway's in gridlock without any noise.

The big trucks and cars like an army of ants
keep crawling the clover-leaf maze of concrete
that looks like a ribbon most carelessly flung.
Your eyes have experienced a wonderful treat.

Then suddenly things look so large they are real.
The wheels hit the runway, the brakes loudly squeal
like rumbling thunder it taxis, then stops.
I bet you'll be thinking that flying is tops.

Anabel LeFrancois

THE KANGAROO

Lets take some time to think about
the awkward kangaroo.
With front legs short and hind legs long
he looks quite strange to me and you.

Did God mix up the body parts?
The hind legs that He made were strong
but legs in front too short to match
the hind legs that He made too long.

But God is wise, He had a plan,
a clever gift He would bestow,
a furry pouch to cuddle babes.
that's why He made the front legs low.

The pouch has gained so much prestige
we mortals manufacture them
to keep our babies close and warm
we parents find the pouch a gem.

When kangaroos get legs in gear
unbalanced though they seem to be,
a thirty mile per hour run
would be a graceful sight to see.

He slips into a biped bounce
in over-drive equipped to go

Me Too, My Friend

    expending no more energy
at speeds real high or speeds quite low.

    The end of his long tail can bend
      just like a boomerang it acts
    to counter balance, keep on keel.
    These fascinating skills are facts.

    And when he wants to take a rest
      he kinda sits upon his tail,
      he uses it much like a stool
    and then continues on his trail.

    The kangaroo's astonishing
     so if the animal looks odd
with front legs short and hind legs long
    remember he's a work of God
        and He knows
                  what
                        He's
                            doing.

Anabel LeFrancois

THE ANIMAL WHO LIVES UPSIDE DOWN

They call him a sloth because he appears
to be sluggish and lazy and slow.
In fact that's the truth, but sometimes he gets
rather agile avoiding a foe.

He lives in the forest, hangs on to the limbs
of the trees and his claws are like hooks,
a frozen hard grip adhering like glue.
He resembles a door mat in looks.

He moves upside down, he sleeps upside down
and he rarely descends to the ground.
He finds it too hard to crawl on his feet
so it's always in trees that he's found.

It takes lots of time to see if he moves,
when it happens it's usually night.
How does he resist the gravity pull
always hanging so long and so tight?

He only sees sky, his head's in the clouds
for his diet, it's leaves and young shoots
occasionally lucky in finding some fruit.
How would you like to be in his boots?

The sloth is as big as any large cat
and quite grayish and coarse is his hair.
He blends with the foliage, algae collects
on his body from damp forest air.

Me Too, My Friend

The green disappears when weather is dry
and there isn't much more to be said
except that he's inoffensive and dull,
he's silent, he's boring, half-dead.

There's only one place on the earth where he thrives,
It's the tropics where climate is mild,
exclusively South America's claim.
He'd never survive in the wild.

He looks like he's much too tired to mate
but he must cause the sloth is still here.
New babies keep coming, a-hanging on trees,
its unlikely that he'll disappear.

He lacks all the charm of panda's and pets
but admire his patience and "cool".
We'd be better to copy the sloth
and think twice before acting the fool.

If God should decide to send us a flood
and the water was rising too high
without any Noah to build us an ark
would you envy the sloth? So would I.
Note: Where did the expression "hanging in there"
come from? The sloth?

Anabel LeFrancois

THE BIRD THAT CAN'T FLY

The penguin's delightful, a marvelous bird
so quaintly amusing it borders on "nerd."
When God made the penguin what was His wish?
Which way was He going, a bird or a fish?
Was God so exhausted He couldn't decide
on which body parts He'd want to provide?
He must have been rushed, not up to His best
the Sabbath was coming, He needed a rest.
The penguin was started, complete it He would
and since He was God did the best that He could.
He crafted small wings and a thick chunky bod,
if a bird was to happen those wings would be odd.
T'would be painful to see the poor thing try flight
so God kept on working far into the night.
The legs turned out shorter than they ought to be
It's wabbling walk was funny to see.
said God to Himself, "I'm not being fair
I'll figure out something, I'm God and I care."
With the snap of a finger He knew what to do
said "I'll give it charisma and charm that is new
to the animal kingdom, I'll make it unique."
Then He set about molding an upward turned beak.
So it wouldn't freeze on the cold arctic shore
He made feathers much finer than ever before.
He decided the colors should be black and white
and arranged them with skill till He got it just right.
The world's first tuxedo gave the penguin it's style.

Me Too, My Friend

For centuries they'd be sure to beguile
with their debonair look and demeanor of pride
they're forever endearing with that ludicrous stride.
Half-breed, mismatched from its head to its toes
that adorable, lovable, popular bird
is smugly content though it's image is blurred.
It can't fly in the sky so it swims in the sea,
makes the best of the worst, here's a lesson that we
should learn from the penguin; Cut out useless stewing
Trust in God who unfailingly knows what He's doing.
The penguin has shown us the essence of magic
and a world without penguins would surely be tragic.

Anabel LeFrancois

THE HORSE THAT IS A FISH

Unlike a fish, the sea horse seems
to look more like a chess board knight
with head and neck more like a horse,
he navigates and swims upright,
quite slowly and with dignity
the rapid movement of the fin
upon his back gets him around,
propels him out of scrapes he's in.

His bony body is encased
with ridge-like plates and studded spines.
His tail is curly, very long
for grasping objects that he twines

and holds on tightly with his tail.
The mouth is tiny and it's at
the very end of his long snout
and furthermore, would you guess that

his eyes work independently?
Do you think you could do that too
and act the clown with funny looks?
I'll tell you things you never knew

about the sea horse and his mate.
The husband has a little pouch,
the wife lays eggs in it to hatch
for forty days plus five, then ouch!

Me Too, My Friend

They're born and they cannot come back
because the opening's too small
so they must fend all by themselves
and learn to hide in sea weed tall

from enemies who also share
their world upon the ocean floor.
Would you believe the babies born
are three-eighths of an inch, no more?

And that's too large for them to go
back in again their daddy's pouch.
Almost two hundred babes expelled
all born at once and I would vouch

survival rate is very low
for these small fish who never get
to reach full growth which is a foot.
They're food for larger fish, I bet.

They live in warm and temperate zones
and there are fifty species known.
Some only grow two inches long,
now wouldn't that be fun to own?

The home aquarium is not
his favorite habitat. They need
the freshened current of the sea,
minutest creatures for their feed.

Alas, they're meant to live down deep
they search for leaf-like growths and hide.
Sea horses fascinate us all
are much admired far and wide.

In each art form that's known to man
they've challenged artists to create
their likeness with their graceful charm,
this horsy fish we celebrate.

THE SAD SAGA OF A TREE

It's time to face reality
that of the blue spruce tree
it can be said
the tree is dead.
There is no doubt
it should come out.
An eyesore so embarrassing
is getting comments questioning
wondering when we
will pull the tree.

But grandpa went to bed and snored.
His wife's appeals he has ignored.
Says he "It's best to stand a while."
The blight of our great landscape plan
he's watering with the seaweed can.
He'll realize in God's good time
the tree will never reach it's prime.

The mailman said "Seaweed will fail,
just make a sign that reads FOR SALE
and hang it on the ailing tree"
delighted with his trickery.

When Grandpa said, "Who thought of this?"
I said, "Not I" in playful bliss.
It stood for days, sad and forlorn
and lost more needles in a storm.

Anabel LeFrancois

Incredible as it may be
there was a "taker" for the tree.
They pinned a dollar to a limb;
who's perpetrator of this whim?

The tree still stands, it's branches hold
a sign that says the tree is sold.
But Grandpa stroked his beard and said,
"I'm not convinced the tree is dead."

He tried all cures, it was no use,
he couldn't save that prized blue spruce.
he finally dug it out and then
your Grandma said "The next time when

you take off for the race track get
that dollar on a long shot bet;
here's hoping for a lucky win."
The horse he picked was fifth one in.

This story grows from week to week.
To our surprise one morning bleak
we found a firmly planted cross
where our tree stood to mourn our loss.

It had a marker "Rest in peace."
These pranks were too much fun to cease.
We honor grave sites so I got
some flowers and a red clay pot.

Me Too, My Friend

A sympathetic card arrived
to say they're sad the tree had died.
The dollar's gone, the tree is out
but that's not what this is about.

Things happen and what's done is done
we found a way to make some fun;
besides a tree so bare and lean
will be just right for Halloween.

COMPENSATION

Mother earth is a woman
with a fat torso.
The sky is her face
the ocean her hair
the weather, her moods.
What about legs?
She doesn't need them,
She gets around
on her axis.

Anabel LeFrancois

C.J. AND HIS TROMBONE

Notes to play and songs to sing
music is a wondrous thing.
In the shiny brass you blow
some notes fast and some notes slow.
Nimble fingers push the keys
coaxing sounds to grow with ease.
Stretch that arm and do a slide
make it smooth and make it glide
into melodies that swell
then, diminish put a spell
in our hearts and in our souls.
When the drums make thunder rolls
those crescendos are a blast
but they're never meant to last.
When the teacher gives the sign
tone it down to soft and fine.
Stay in tune and keep the beat
if it helps you, tap your feet.
When you're playing Sousa's march
give it spirit, zip and starch.
Read your notes as fast you can
keep one eye on Music Man.
Doing all these things at once
can't be done by any dunce.
It's a challenge, that's for sure
but you're C.J. you'll endure
scales and practice are a bore

Me Too, My Friend

blowing till your lips are sore
give it time, you're bound to find
that it's not an endless grind.
Making music is great fun
giving joy to everyone.
Notes to play and songs to sing
Music is a wondrous thing.

Anabel LeFrancois

ESCAPADE OF A CAT

There was a cat with reddish fur
I don't remember, him or her.
One day it came to Grandma's home
and settled down, no more to roam.
They lived in peace and harmony
until one day when she said we
should have a cat, a cat is neat
without a cat we're not complete.
She said because she planned to be
up Spokane way with family.
So that is how we got a cat
called "Tabby" who was puzzled at
the going's on of lots of boys
who constantly made lots of noise.

Then one day in the family room
cat almost met ill-fated doom.
If cats all have nine lives, that's luck.
When boys played pool, cat ran amuck
and jumped upon the table top.
It happened much too fast to stop;
chased rolling balls both to and fro
as fast as it's four legs would go.
The boys laughed hard, t'was strange to see.
The crazy cat was frantically
pursuing balls and chased one through
a pocket hole, the boys withdrew

Me Too, My Friend

their cue sticks, paused, and then they heard
a scared meeoow! It was absurd.
Time seemed to drag and all was still.
The boys began to wonder will
they have to take the thing apart?
They didn't think the cat was smart.
How would they get the dumb cat out?
But Tabby found another route,
another hole, up popped a head
surprised, perplexed, a look of dread
with ears alert, eyes open wide
took swiveled looks from side to side.
Oh! What a sight, what comedy,
the boys all laughed hilariously.
Soon after that, cat ran away
to find a safer place to stay.
Though years have passed, it is a fact
no cat put on a better act.

VALENTINE

The origin of valentine
is shrouded in much mystery.
It goes back many centuries
and has a lengthy history.

There are two theories, I have read
that are intriguing, that's for sure
the charming custom caught on fast
and through the ages did endure.

In ancient times the Romans planned
a spring fertility affair,
the celebration lasted days,
for parties Romans had a flair.

Young maidens wrote love notes to men
and dropped them in an urn, hoped fate
would prompt the guys to pick them up
then court them and they'd get a mate.

In medieval times belief
that when the birds began to nest
in February, perhaps man
should put that theory to a test.

Me Too, My Friend

Love smitten young men grabbed the chance
and started to send love notes to
someone they viewed romantically
desired to pursue and woo.

Some archaeologist unearthed
a catacomb and further search
revealed a fascinating find,
the ruins of an ancient church.

T'was dedicated to a saint
a holy priest named Valentine
who suffered martyrdom and then
was canonized and called divine.

A scholar found reports that proved
there lived another by that name
both martyred on the very day
we celebrate this feast of fame.

One was a bishop, one a priest,
it matters not, the legacy
they left behind we can't dispute
they taught us how we ought to be.

The paper valentines appeared
about five hundred years ago
like "Won't you be my Valentine?"
and tell me that you won't say "No."

Then enterprising Yankees thought
"Here is a money making scheme."
In 1840 factory cards
then hit the market with their "theme."
I've often wondered who first drew
angelic angels with a bow
and arrow that he aimed at hearts
but I suppose I'll never know.

In modern times kids go to school
all loaded up with cards to share
with corny rhymes and silly puns
to tell their classmates that they care.

Their daddies scratch their heads and hope
they'll come up with a thought that's neat.
Their mothers hope that they will too
and that he'll take them out to eat.

It is a day for happenings
proposals and engagement rings,
a day for loving one and all,
good feelings that our loving brings.
Oh what a happy day!
We thank you dear St. Valentine.

Me Too, My Friend

MAKING LEMONADE

An electric transformer
disgraced our front yard.
It was gray, drab and metal,
on the eyes it was hard.
This ugly disaster
was a really bum rap
so your Grandma got out
her "smart thinking cap."
I'd make something happen
this could not be delayed.
We nailed boards around it
put on roofing for shade,
made a little white window
a planter for flowers.
Adding white picket fencing
kept us busy for hours.
A sign saying "GUEST HOUSE"
and a shiny brass bell,
posies spilling from planters
had their story to tell.
The folks who were passing
the once ugly sight
found the transformer hidden
and no longer a blight.
T'was a month before Xmas
it came to me strong
Santa needed a workshop

Anabel LeFrancois

how could I go wrong?
So a Santa with helpers,
his reindeer and lights
brought cheer to the scene
and sparkled dark nights.
T'was fun and when Xmas
was over and done
it was again GUEST HOUSE
another rerun.

Then with Valentine coming
and "toujour l'amour"
a heart family stood grinning
with Cupid's allure.

Then came March and St Patrick
and cute leprechauns
mischievous in clover.
In April it dons
the spring trappings of Easter.
When summer arrived
the theme was a barnyard
like a real countryside.

In October it's haunted
with Halloween ghosts.
With Thanksgiving coming
folks buy turkeys to roast.
The next story will tell you
of November's display.

Me Too, My Friend

Old MacDonald was resting
on a big bale of hay.

Then we're back to December
with Santa in sight.
Merry Christmas to all
and to all a Good Night.

When Life Give You Lemons  **Be Smart and Make Lemonade**

Anabel LeFrancois

GRANDMOTHER'S THANKSGIVING DECORATION

That little house in our front yard
is all decked out a different way.
November's here, the air has chilled
we'll celebrate Thanksgiving Day.

Let's play a game and visualize
the many things that I have done.
I'll paint a picture all with words
to tell about your Grandma's fun.

There stands a cornstalk, pumpkin large,
a harvest with some squash,
the window shows a horse's head
a-nibbl'in on some corn, by gosh!

A turkey over two feet tall
is holding up a sign that shows
he's scared and hopes this year you'll try
a ham instead and quell his woes.

A mama piggy and her babe
are looking for a hiding place,
they'd like to be invisible
and disappear without a trace.

Alas their little curly tails
and upturned snouts are showing through
the peeky holes in junipers.
Poor piggies don't know what to do.

Me Too, My Friend

And now I'll tell the big surprise.
Old Santa is reclined upon
a bale of straw, holds cider jug.
I hear you say, "Don't put me on."

He's smiling, waving to the folks
a-passing by, they're unaware
that Santa Claus is dressed up in
my painting clothes and orange yarn hair.

With old straw hat and farmer shoes
he's Old MacDonald, that's for sure,
contented with his corn cob pipe
and harvest yield he feels secure.

The autumn leaves around the house
are bright and colorful to see.
A sign says Old MacDonald hopes
you'll spend Thanksgiving happily.

The folks who go by Grandma's house
don't know that Santa is inside
of Old MacDonald, they are fooled
but to my grandson I'll confide.
I've fooled the people, everyone,
your grandma's having lots of fun.

Anabel LeFrancois

HOW CLEVER IS THE BOOMERANG

How clever is the boomerang
and also scientific,
it's true this soaring man-made fang
has qualities terrific.

The humble aborigines
discovered that an angle
when whittled at 90 degrees
cut air with speed and twangle
and if the target isn't hit
returns itself to sender.
This service is, you must admit,
incredible to render.

This throwing stick earns good review
has value for the poet,
philosophers and preachers too
who were the first to know it;
inventing hosts of metaphors,
to score their points with cunning
in literary corridors
each other they're out running.

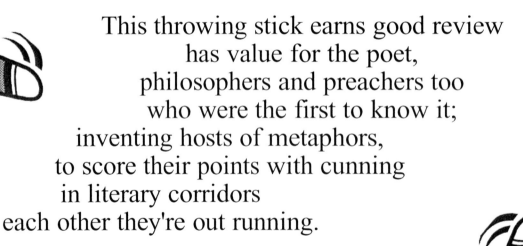

The missile, salmon, boomerang,
the pigeon and the yo yo
somehow all have a built in skill
for orbiting their go go.
The boomerang is awesome.

Me Too, My Friend

A PUZZLE FOR C.J.

There's something in sagebrush
besides food for bees
and mundane odd uses,
the plant is a tease.

There's more to the sagebrush,
I've felt it for years,
a cure for an illness
to conquer our fears.

This shrub has been waiting
for someone to find
it's magical potion
that could be combined

with something or other
who knows what it is?
It may be a substance
that scientists miss.

New uses for sagebrush
that are now obscure
could just be the breakthrough
much needed to cure.

Could you be the genius
who figures it out?

Anabel LeFrancois

I leave you this puzzle
what is it about?

The sagebrush has cluttered
up much of the earth,
since it's so abundant
it must have some worth

because
God always knows
what He's doing.

Me Too, My Friend

IT'S MY FAULT

From the oven there's seeping
an odor that's reeking.
It piggy backs air waves
all over the house
then glides through the screens
in an effort to douse
the afternoon air
that's drowsy and basking
in warm summer sun.
In case you are asking
it's degree of success,
half way down the block
would be a good guess.
Soon nostrils familiar
with the wonderful smell
arrive at my doorstep
as though summoned by bell.
They tell me it's my fault,
nobody ignores
the fact that I stunk up
all of outdoors.
As I cut crusty ends
from the warm bread that stinks
the kids say their grateful
for the good smell that finks.

Anabel LeFrancois

DOGS

For thousands of years the faithful dog
has helped share the workload of man.
With an inborn sense he relates to us
and our lives intertwine with his clan.
His heroic deeds are recorded in books.
He thrives on our praise and when scolded feels bad.
He's unique, a member of family to us;
when he dies we're incredibly sad.
He's playmate to children, their cuddly pet
talks with barks, his whines and affectionate licks.
He'll learn many tricks and perform on command,
bring the paper, retrieve balls and sticks;
he likes chasing cats, all things moving and cars,
likes barking dog chases, should fighting occur,
for a piece of the action he's game
though the price may be blood and some fur.
Now he's not being naughty or cruel,
stimulation likes that is a blast.
It's an instinct that's built in his genes
he's adhering to ways of the past.
On close observation you'll find
that he's careful in choosing his space.
Before laying down he will go round and round
like his ancestors staking home base
in tall grasses of primeval times.
The gospel of caution is carved in cement.
If feeling unsafe he will roll in the dirt;

Me Too, My Friend

he's destroying his bodily scent.
His sense of alertness is sharpened and keen,
for him flight or fight must be handled alone.
A habit still lingers from primitive times;
he'll go to much trouble to bury a bone.
His sense of direction is envied by man
no matter the distance he'll find his way back.
Loud noises are painful assaults to his ears,
firecrackers a brutal attack.
We've all heard him howl in the still of the night
he's calling his mate cause he's lonesome and blue
the sound is so mournfully sad and we hope
that wherever she is she'll hear him too.
We know dogs have feelings that run very deep
he's our friend and we care when he's troubled or ill,
he's the greatest companion that a body could have
and loyal to the core with a heart of good will,
a favorite pet,
we're all in his debt.

Note: When primitive man began taming wild dogs there were only a few different breeds to be found. The strong and the muscular pulled heavy loads and some were skilled at protecting a flock. Some had a heightened sense of smell and they were used for the hunt. By now the breeds have been divided into six groups: working dogs, sporting dogs, hounds, non-sporting dogs, terriers and toys.

Anabel LeFrancois

GOD INVENTED FUN

God of monkeys, gooney birds
pelicans and chimpanzees,
waddling penguins, barking seals
friendly dogs and cats who tease,

dolphins with amusing smiles
parrots who talk back to us,
horses, bunnies, kangaroos
all can be ridiculous.

Bible studies say that God
made the animals in twos.
In that long enduring task
I believe He left us clues,

manifesting that he has
so much humor in His heart
that he made some animals
very playful and quite smart.

"Humanness" was meant to be
"bonding glue" for beast and man
to each other we'd relate.
Was that not a clever plan?

Animals are fun to watch,
every species has it's style;
they're companions, pets and friends,
with their antics they beguile.

Me Too, My Friend

It is fortunate for us
that the way something was said
or a happening occurred
strikes us funny in the head

triggering a belly laugh.
It's so obvious that God's
sense of humor is superb.
Always thought it rather odd

sermons never focused on
this attractive attribute.
Why do I feel so alone
messaging my gratitude?

DRACULA'S CASTLE

Years ago your grandmother traveled through
Romania. In the hills of Translyvania a castle
stands tall on a lofty rocky mound. From all
sides one sees many miles of mountainous
terrain, lush multicolored vegetation spread
out like a huge patch quilt. It's many balconies
and windows belie the fact that it's more
like a fort designed to spot an enemy's
approach in days before gunpowder was
invented. Five hundred years ago a prince lived
here and ruled with cruelty; his subjects lived
in constant fear. He was not invented for
scary Halloween stories. He was a real prince
with normal looks. Those ugly rubber masks
turn him inside out and reveal a very sick
mind. It felt creepy going through dreary,
dingy rooms, spooky narrow passageways
with low ceilings, and the musty dungeon he
filled with prisoners made me sad. I wished
the castle was really a castle and that
Dracula had never lived. I couldn't wait to get
out in fresh air and bright sunshine. In my
memory is etched one of the most awesome
landscapes I've ever seen with a castle that
serenely sentinels centuries of time.

Me Too, My Friend

THE MAN IN THE MOON

He may look handsome from earth, shimmering
silvery reflections in the night's sky,
luring flirtatious would be moon bride stars,
but he'll never see his billionth birthday
again, he's crusty and dusty, and he's as wide
as from Cleveland to San Francisco. He has
chronic acne, more than 30,000 scars and pits,
20,000 ft. deep and some towering peaks of 26,000 ft.
but what can you expect
from a diet of moldy green cheese? He's
really to be pitied. In his world gravity is
weak, atmosphere thin, moisture scant and
he has no light of his own. So what does he
do? Keeping a respectable distance of some
210,000 miles he travels an oval orbit
around Mother Earth at a fast clip of 2300
mph. That speed really impressed my sons
until three men in a corning ware cone cut
space at 25,000 mph. We disillusioned ourselves
when we invaded his privacy. With his
assortment of many moons from crescent to
full, harvest moons and blue moons, he was
meant to be enjoyed from afar. Let's give the
moon back to the little people like romantic
songwriters, lovers and poets.

CIRCLE CHOICES

Once upon a time there was a nice, long straight line whose beginning and end got caught up in quarreling. They arched their spines, became deadlocked in getting even with each other. Their quarreling became a habit that kept repeating itself. That is how the vicious circle came to be which gave birth to problems that caused worry that also thinks in circles. So, meanness creates more meanness. That's the bad news about circles.

On the other hand, once there was a nice straight line whose beginning and end got caught up in a mutual friendship and they reached out to each other. Their kindness to each other bent and encircled all the goodness in their happy lives. They became molded in their harmonious togetherness and that is how the first halo came to be. So, a halo is made of acts of kindness that inspire more acts of kindness and makes us happy. That's the good news about circles.

Me Too, My Friend

DID YOU KNOW?

That the best things in the whole wide world
are things we cannot see?
They can't be packaged up to sell
to folks like you and me.
The things that matter most to us
are not found in a store.
It's love we give and love received
that moves us to the core.

It's strange but we must realize
that things we cannot buy
in wrappings and take home with us
all have a price that's high.
Now, self-respect and self-esteem
and peace of mind within ourselves
come only with good deeds.

That feeling of accomplishment
we get when work is done
is gratifying, it's because
another battle's won.
The happiness that's genuine
lives in a giving heart.
We must not let the "grumpies" in
to tear us all apart.

There's empathy and sympathy
we give to those in pain
a chance to prove we've got "right stuff"
and give without self-gain.
Our sensitivity provides
ability to "feel"
yet we can't hear or see or touch
or photograph what's real.

For feelings you rely on words
to let the doctor know
what hurts, express your deepest thoughts
of joy and tales of woe.
These thoughts are deep but you are smart
and know the golden rule.
I think you sense that reaching out
to others makes you "cool."

Your Grandma's lived a long, long time
and likes to think things through,
she hopes that these amazing facts
are interesting to you.

When you are bored, just make a list
of things you cannot see,
you'll be surprised how very long
it might turn out to be.

THINK ABOUT IT

The cave man spoke with guttural grunts, with his hands and body. Gradually man invented more words for communicating with others. Through many centuries more and more words were invented in many languages. They tell us to spell check in our computers hold 50,000 words. Think about the first courageous people who got the idea to put them all together in one book with definitions, origins and pronunciations. The Oxford Dictionary appeared in the late 1800's and took 70 years to complete. It had over 400,000 words. Spelling and looking up words can be a bore but the study of words can be fascinating. Writing is playing with words and making rhymes is a real head game. Why not try making up little rhymes about your life, your feelings and things you see? Think about how happy it would make you feel to give your parents little poems just to tell them you love them. They would treasure your poems more than anything from card racks. Don't be afraid to try and don't give up trying or you'll never know how good you might be. Good Luck.

Table of Contents

AND THAT'S THE WAY IT IS 2

A BOOK IS BORN 4

BE GOOD TO YOURSELF 5

LIVING THROUGH A MAGNIFYING GLASS 6

THE BEGINNER'S LAMENT 7

THE MANY FACES OF PATIENCE 8

S-T-R-E-T-C-H 9

CHEER UP, THINGS COULD BE WORSE 10

A VERY DEEP THOUGHT 10

THANKSGIVING 11

SLEEP 12

AWAKING 13

CONSIDERING 14

DEALING WITH MY MORALITY 15

MORNING PRAYER 15

SPRING 16

DENIAL 17

THE DENTIST 18

A NO WIN 18

ON MOWING THE LAWN 19

MY LUCKY HERITAGE 20

PICTURE 21

LOSS 22

PARABLE OF COURAGE 22

FOR MACULAR DEGENERATES LIKE ME 23

THE BATHROOM NIGHT LIGHT 23

WHEN WILL I GROW UP? 24

ON BEING UPTIGHT 24

PROBLEM SOLVING 25

I GUESS IT'S CALLED MATURITY 26

MY DAUGHTER"S PERSIAN CAT 27

VALUES 29

THE BOTTOM LINE 30

WHAT GOES AROUND COMES AROUND 31

WHY NOT? 31

POWER STRIPES 32

REMEMBER WHEN 33

METHUSELAH MUSINGS 34

METHUSELAH 35

A PHILOSOPHICAL BIRTHDAY WISH 36

DOES ANYBODY KNOW? 36

MY THINK TANK, THE DISH PAN 37

RECOLLECTIONS 38

THE SENIOR MOMENT CLUB 39

CANDLELIGHT 39

ODE TO A MOUSE'S EAR 40

NOTHING 41

A VERY SMALL INCIDENT 41

THE PERILS OF PAULINE 42

TRIGGERINGS 43

LET ME RUN AWAY 44

MS. MIRACLE GROW 46

TRUE CONFESSIONS 47

A GET WELL WISH 48

REMINISCING 49

MY FRIEND 50

THE ELLUSIVE TRUTH 51

SOMETHING TO THINK ABOUT 51

MARIN VALLEY'S PANORAMIC GIFT 52

A HARD WORKING RETIREE 53

THINGS THAT MAKE MY DAY 54

THE BRIDESMAID 55

THE QUAIL FAMILY 56

THE APPLE 57

ESSAY OF HIS OFFSPRING 58

ANOTHER ESSAY 58

HAPPY BIRTHDAY 59

WHAT IF 60

SHE LIVED TO BE ONE HUNDRED 61

WISDOM 62

MY HOBBY 63

THAT WAS THEN, THIS IS NOW 64

MY TOTEM POLE 65

MAKING SENSE OF FAILURES 66

AN UNFORGETTABLE MAN 67

EVERYBODY HAS THEIR STORY 69

METAMORPHOSIS 70

A GOOD THING TO FORGET 71

AFTERTHOUGHTS 71

FOR SALE 72

AN OVERHEARD REFRESHING RESPONSE 72

TODAY I PLAYED CARPENTER 73

DISCIPLINE 74

MAKING ADJUSTMENTS .75

Anabel LeFrancois

HAPPY HEAD 76
CARTOON 77
A PRAYER 78
SAYISMS 79
FAVORITE QUOTES 80
INCORRIGIBLE 81
FAITH IN HOPE 81
THE WISHING WELL 82
PRAYER OF ST. FRANCIS OF ASSISI 83
EPILOGUE 84

Poems for Grandchildren

INTRODUCTION 87
A FANTASY TRIP 88
EASTER EGG HUNT 89
A CHILD'S WISH 90
WHY DO TOES WRINKLE IN THE TUB? 91
DO CATS HAVE BELLY BUTTONS? 92
THE CUTE STINKY SKUNK 93
MONKEYS 94
THREE LEGGED CAT 94
DO GOATS REALLY EAT TIN CANS? 95
THE TURTLE 96
A LOVE AFFAIR 97
A TRUE BEDTIME STORY 99
THE PELICAN 101
IS THE OWL REALLY WISE 102
FLYING HIGH 104
THE KANGAROO 106

Me Too, My Friend

THE ANIMAL WHO LIVES UPSIDE DOWN 108

THE BIRD THAT CAN'T FLY 110

THE HORSE THAT IS A FISH 112

THE SAD SAGA OF A TREE 115

COMPENSATION 117

C.J. AND HIS TROMBONE 118

ESCAPADE OF A CAT 120

VALENTINE 122

MAKING LEMONADE 125

GRANDMOTHER'S THANKSGIVING DECORATION 128

THE BOOMERANG 130

A PUZZLE FOR C.J. 131

IT'S MY FAULT 133

DOGS 134

GOD INVENTED FUN 136

DRACULA'S CASTLE 138

THE MAN IN THE MOON 139

CIRCLE CHOICES 140

DID YOU KNOW? 141

THINK ABOUT IT 143